4-4-96@

Letting the lantern fall, Libby made ready to take advantage of the hesitancy being shown by the Texan. She darted forward and sent her right foot into the air with the kind of precision she had demonstrated when kicking open the French windows of Countess Olga Simonouski's suite at the Grand Republic Hotel in Washington, D.C. What's more, her aim was good enough to achieve her purpose.

Caught under the jaw with considerable force, the Kid's head snapped back and he pitched over with bright lights erupting in his skull.

However, as the Texan was going down, his forefinger instinctively tightened on the trigger of the Dragoon and it went off thunderously.

"And I know what Betty Hardin 'n' Belle Boyd can do with their feet!" was the Kid's last conscious thought as he sprawled supine on the ground. "I'll *never* hear the end of this."

Books by J. T. Edson

THE NIGHTHAWK
NO FINGER ON THE TRIGGER
THE BAD BUNCH
SLIP GUN
TROUBLED RANGE
THE FASTEST GUN IN TEXAS
THE HIDE AND TALLOW MEN
THE JUSTICE OF COMPANY Z
McGRAW'S INHERITANCE
RAPIDO CLINT
COMANCHE
A MATTER OF HONOR
RENEGADE
WACO RIDES IN
BLOODY BORDER
ALVIN FOG, TEXAS RANGER
HELL IN THE PALO DURO
OLE DEVIL AT SAN JACINTO
GO BACK TO HELL
OLE DEVIL AND THE MULE TRAIN
VIRIDIAN'S TRAIL
OLE DEVIL AND THE CAPLOCKS
TO ARMS! TO ARMS, IN DIXIE!
TEXAS FURY
THE SOUTH WILL RISE AGAIN
BUFFALO ARE COMING
MARK COUNTER'S KIN

TEXAS
KIDNAPPERS

J. T. EDSON

A DELL BOOK

Published by
Dell Publishing
a division of
Bantam Doubleday Dell Publishing Group, Inc.
1540 Broadway
New York, New York 10036

ISBN: 0-440-22213-3

Printed in the United States of America

Published simultaneously in Canada

March 1996

10 9 8 7 6 5 4 3 2 1

RAD

For Carol, my favorite Civil Servant,
plus my sons, Peter and Mark, all of
whom have the great good taste to share
my high regard for Chuck Norris, but
Carol is not so keen on Matilda the Hun.

Author's Note

Although we originally told all we knew about the events recorded herein as Part Two, "The Quartet," *The Half-Breed,* further details have been received from Alvin Dustine "Cap" Fog that allow us to produce the full story behind the kidnapping of Elizabeth "Betty" Hardin.

For the benefit of new readers, but to save our old hands from repetition, we have given a "potted biography" of Belle "the Rebel Spy" Boyd and the Ysabel Kid in the form of Appendixes.

When supplying us with the information from which we produce our books, one of the strictest rules imposed upon us by the present-day members of what we call the "Hardin, Fog and Blaze" clan and the "Counter" family is that we *never* under *any* circumstances disclose their true identities or their current whereabouts. Furthermore, we are instructed to *always* include sufficient inconsistencies to ensure that neither can happen even inadvertently.

We would like to emphasize that the names of people who appear in this volume are those supplied to us by our informants in Texas and any resemblance to those of other people, living or dead, is purely coincidental.

We realize that, in our present "permissive" society, we could use the actual profanities employed by various people in the narrative. However, unlike various other authors, we do not concede that a spurious desire to create "realism" is any excuse for doing so.

As we refuse to pander to the current trendy usage of the metric system, except when referring to the caliber of various firearms that had always been measured in milli-meters—i.e., Walther P-38, 9mm—we will continue to employ miles, yards, feet, inches, pounds, and ounces when quoting distances and weights.

Lastly, and of the *greatest* importance, we must stress that the attitudes and speech of the characters are put down as would have been the case at the period of this narrative.

J. T. EDSON,
MELTON MOWBRAY,
Leics.,
England.

CHAPTER ONE

IT'S JUST LIKE SHE SAID
IT WOULD BE

Rising four stories in height, with extensive cellars underneath wherein were situated among other facilities the
mechanism for operating the hydraulic elevators allowing
all except the uppermost one to be reached without the
guests having to climb stairs, there was considerable justification for the claim by the Grand Republic Hotel to be
the largest, best-situated, and most luxurious establishment
of its kind in Washington, D.C., and up to the standards
of the finest in any other country's major cities.

Being comprised of delicacies from around the world as
well as those found only in the United States, the food and
beverages were of a first-rate standard of excellence and
prepared and served by an exceptionally well-trained staff.
The waiters and waitresses in the magnificent main dining
area and smaller rooms where meals of a less public nature
could be taken were trained to perfection and, like the rest
of the domestic personnel, noted for their discretion. Chosen for their size and bearing, being attired in garments of
military cut of a kind that had gone out of use except for
ceremonial purposes in the United States Army, the door-
men could supply information about most matters pertain-
ing to the capital city and its environment, particularly

those of a confidential nature such as where various types of diversion or company could be located. It was rumored that the amount each received as gratuities for his services, especially those of the latter variety, made his salary seem a mere pittance.

Furthermore, the services offered for the protection of the guests' property had often been praised. Those who wished to do so could leave their surplus money and jewelry in a box that could only be opened by two keys. One was for the possession of the owner and the other was held in a locked steel cupboard, which the duty manager alone could open in his permanently occupied office. The precautions taken were considered a matter of the gravest importance by the management.

From the beginning, the Grand Republic had received custom from the wealthiest families in the United States, whether involved in railroads, internal or overseas shipping, mining of precious metals or coal, or the cattle industry, which had brought prosperity back to a Texas left impoverished by supporting the Confederacy in the Civil War and was now starting to do the same in other states.[1] Furthermore, since its fame had spread worldwide by word of mouth, it was regarded as *de rigueur* for such foreign dignitaries who did not receive private accommodation in the capital city to stay there. Although many of the latter brought personal servants, for whom quarters of a lower standard were available on the upper of the four floors, albeit not served by the elevator, all levels of the workforce were carefully selected for competence at their duties and honesty.

To ensure that the latter quality was possessed, nobody was hired without a careful check being made upon their antecedents to ensure they would be trustworthy. Furthermore, the management maintained two efficient former peace officers and a female attendant, who was equally conversant with her duties, on the premises at all times in the capacity of what a later generation would call house detectives. Between them, being able to recognize many confidence tricksters, crooked gamblers, and other members of the criminal fraternity, they were able to keep such undesirables from operating on the premises. There was another part of their duties that was a most effective deterrent to petty or more serious pilfering on the part of the workforce. Not being offered protection by the restrictions that organizers of labor unions of a later day would refuse to permit, regardless of the justification for them being required, even the desk clerks and other senior members of the staff were compelled to don garments of a uniform nature and indicative of each's status in the hierarchy of the hotel supplied to them on arriving for duty and, regardless of the position held, should there be cause would have their own clothing and persons searched before they were allowed to leave.

Because of the high standard of security employed at the hotel, it was generally assumed by the management and the city's law-enforcement agencies that a robbery there was impossible to perpetrate.

However, that theory was soon to be disproved in no uncertain fashion.

What was more, the theft was to be carried out from what—despite having some possibilities for allowing unwanted access—was considered to be the safest part of the whole building.

Serving as a storage area for trunks and other items not required in the rooms by the occupants, the roof of the hotel rose in an inverted V. However, around it was what amounted to a wide balcony allowing maintenance work to be carried out. It was well known that the decorative and protective wooden barrier was only a safety measure during the hours of daylight. Each evening, one of the—although the term had not yet come into usage—security force went up and set free the securing bolts that had kept in a nominally safe condition on being replaced at dawn. Doing so allowed it to turn outward on well-oiled hinges if leaned or otherwise pulled upon, and its weak construction would prevent it from supporting any except the lightest of weights. This precaution was intended to prevent the barrier from being used as a means of descending by a ladder or rope to the rooms below, many being fitted with balconies allowing the occupants to go outside and admire the view of their surroundings, but that might otherwise have permitted an unauthorized entrance.

When deciding to steal the extremely valuable jewelry collection brought from Russia by Countess Olga Simonouski, who rumor claimed had less-than-honorable motives for remaining in Washington instead of accompanying her husband on a hunting expedition west of the Mississippi River, Libby Craddock had been all too aware of the difficulties to be encountered. However, by virtue of her upbringing and being possessed of no scruples or fear of possible danger, she had refused to be deterred by considerations of the risks involved. Putting her highly developed skills as an organizer to use, she had found the means by which an entry to the suite occupied by her intended victim could be achieved. With the Countess being absent at a high-society ball and—according to the source of information that had been acquired by one of her confederates—unlikely to be returning until the early hours of the morning, as well as having the good fortune of the weather proving suitable for her needs, she was about to put her scheme into effect.

Standing in the small amount of light given by a three-quarters moon, dressed ready to start the attempt, Libby presented a sight that would have drawn much attention from most masculine eyes. Twenty-five years of age, although she had never lived a life of self-restraint, having the need to keep herself in excellent physical condition, there was little sign of it. Held back by a black scarf, her reddish-brunette hair framed a slightly aquiline face that, although somewhat marred by the coldly calculating glint that never left her hazel eyes—although this was rarely noticed until too late, if at all, by the men upon whom she exerted her undeniable charm for predatory purposes—was currently devoid of makeup and showed the tan acquired by her way of life. Because of the way it was filled, the black leotard that was her sole piece of attire—apart from pumps such as a ballet dancer would use except for not having the well-padded "points" that allow dancing upon the toes for lengthy periods to be performed and a leather belt with a small pouch at the left and an ivory-handled knife with a spear point sheathed on the right—was sensual in the extreme. Close fitting at the neck and between the legs, it clung to her magnificently countered body like a second skin. Exposed by its being sleeveless, her arms had well-developed muscles without these causing any loss to her blatant sexuality.

Clearly being twins about the same age and clad and armed in a similar fashion to Libby, apart from Luigi having a neatly trimmed mustache while Giovanni was clean-shaven albeit always having a dark tint to his olive cheeks that made him appear in need of one, the Martinelli brothers were alike in being tall, lithe, and wiry. When moving, they possessed a catlike grace that was of the greatest benefit for their everyday and present occupation and frequently proved most attractive to women. Making use of the latter trait, it had been Luigi—older of the pair by about half an hour—who procured the most important piece of information, which had allowed the reddish-brunette to decide that the time had come for them to carry out the robbery upon the planning of which she had devoted much attention.

There was nothing lithe or wiry about the fourth member of the group standing on the balcony to which they had gained access by a skylight in the roof. In fact, the appearance presented by Stanislaus Padoubny—although few would have known him by that name—was far from prepossessing. With his close-cropped black hair parted down the center and glistening from a liberal application of bay rum, his heavily mustached face was so brutish in aspect as to be close to frightening. Over six feet in height and built on massive lines that his no more extensive garb showed off, if not to advantage offered to the others, a muscular development well above average.

Especially in the case of Padoubny, arranging to have her companions obtain access to the hotel without being detected had been only one of the problems with which Libby was faced while planning the robbery. However, as with each of the others, she had come up with a solution that worked. Making use of an ability at disguise she had learned from her father, who had performed a highly regarded "quick-change" act on the stage, she had been able to make herself able to pass as a stout Irishwoman employed as a member of the housekeeping staff. Although having passed the scrutiny to which all employees were subjected, Bridget O'Toole was prone to take more than just one nip of whiskey when not on duty.

Having made the woman's acquaintance and studied her sufficiently to be confident the deception would work, as it would not need to be maintained for long and the lateness of the hour rendered the need to mingle with anybody else for any length of time unlikely, Libby had visited her at home and contrived to slip her a drugged drink on the pretense of celebrating a nonexistent sister giving birth to a son. The victim was left in an unconscious state and would not be likely to be discovered before morning, as her husband was working the night shift at his place of employment. Arriving at the hotel, with the leotards under the clothing used for passing unnoticed through the streets—even Padoubny managing to avoid attracting undue attention, having had on the habit of a monk and kept the cowl drawn up to partially conceal his features—Libby had waited for an opportunity to let her companions come in through the entrance. Keeping to the stairs allocated for use by the staff and servants of guests, they had reached the balcony on the roof. Once there, they had removed their outer garments and were now ready for the next vitally important stage of the plan.

While the brothers were carefully and silently allowing a section of the guard rail to hinge forward, Padoubny was unwinding from around his body a manila fiber rope of three-strand construction and laid extra hard for strength and smoothness—of the kind frequently used for making the lariats employed by cowhands in the range country of the West. There was a loop large enough to encircle his torso spliced securely into one end and it had knots at intervals down the remainder of what in a lariat would have been called the stem. Because of his size and bulk, he had been able to carry one of sufficient length for the purposes of the party beneath the monk's habit, now lying with the other temporarily discarded attire, without its being discernible.

Even without being aware that such ropes were capable of holding firm against the strains imposed by the tugging of a full-grown longhorn bull trying to escape when needed in the West, Libby and the brothers were confident it would do what they required. Therefore, when Padoubny had the loop over his shoulder and allowed the remainder to fall downward, she had no qualms as she took hold of the stem. Waiting for the burly man to adopt a position that would allow him to support the weights that would be imposed respectively by herself and each of the twins, she grasped the stem and started the descent with the ease she had acquired, along with several other equally specialized skills she found of use in the more lucrative occupation upon which she was now engaged, during a life spent performing various kinds of acts at circuses.

Aided by the knots made in the rope for that purpose and her excellent physical condition, Libby made the descent through the unrelieved gloom for three floors to the balcony of the suite that she knew was occupied by the Countess. Although the levels above had been in darkness, a chink of light showed through the curtains of the French windows that she knew gave access to the sitting room. However, a peek through the gap assured her it was unoccupied. Satisfied on that vitally important point, she gave the tug on the rope they had arranged to notify the first of the brothers he could join her.

"There's nothing from Jinks to warn us we've been seen," Libby announced, turning from where she was looking downward over the balcony as the first of her associates joined her. Not unexpectedly, being a member of an act called the Flying Lombardos and having performed upon the trapeze at the circus where he and his brother Giovanni had met and been recruited by her, he too had made the descent with no greater difficulty despite having a small bull's-eye lantern hooked on the rear of his waist belt.

"I don't know why you had to fetch *him* along," the older of the twins said petulantly. Although he had never been outside the United States, like his brother he spoke with a pronounced Italian accent. "He's always likely to be noticed, especially hanging around outside a place like this so late at night."

"He's too smart to let himself be noticed and can hide easier than you could," Libby answered, never pleased when any decision she made was questioned. "Besides, he's getting a full cut out of the deal and, even though there was nothing for him to do inside, I figured he might as well do something to earn it."

"It's just like she said it would be," Luigi stated. Concluding he would be advised to let the matter drop, he had crossed to look through the chink in the curtain. Turning his attention in that direction, he tried the handle of the French windows and, finding they held firm, went on, "They're fastened. Can you open them?"

"Of course," Libby declared with certainty, taking a small roll of leather from the pouch on her belt and opening it while there were indications that Giovanni was commencing the descent. "Give me some light."

On the order—and it had been that rather than a request—given by the reddish-brunette being complied with, the light from the lantern showed that the leather had concealed several devices Luigi knew to be the set of lock picks she could operate with skill. Selecting one after having illuminated the keyhole and examined it for a moment, she inserted and started to move it. When this failed to produce any effect, she returned it to the slot from which it was taken and chose another. On this occasion, paying no attention to the arrival of the younger twin or his sibling's telling what had happened sotto voce in their native tongue, which she spoke with reasonable fluency, she met with more success and there was a clicking sound to indicate that the mechanism of the lock had operated. However, when she tried the door, it still refused to open.

"Damn it!" Libby spat out as she replaced the pick and returned the leather container to the pouch. "The top bolt's been fastened."

"What can *you* do, then?" Giovanni growled, never having been enamored of the way in which the reddish-brunette made it plain that she considered herself the dominant partner of their group.

"Is she likely to be in there, Lou?" Libby inquired instead of answering the younger brother's question.

"Not according to what I know of her," the older twin answered, sharing his sibling's sentiments on the subject of the reddish-brunette's attitude. "She wasn't any too pleased when I told her I couldn't take her to the beer garden tonight and said she'd find somebody who would, and I don't reckon she'd have any difficulty in doing that. What're you going to do?"

Once again refraining from supplying information as requested, Libby raised her left foot and, with the deft grace of a ballet dancer—or one experienced in the French hand-and-foot boxing style called *savate*—delivered a sharp kick just above the lock. The noise doing so made was not excessive, but it seemed to be that way to the brothers, and they gazed about them in something close to alarm while each's right hand went to the knife he had sheathed on his belt. Although Libby had contrived to avoid giving any sign of sharing their perturbation, she felt a touch of relief when the impact caused the windows to open. Satisfied with having given another example of her ability to cope with an unanticipated situation, although she had envisaged something of the sort might arise, she parted the curtain and, without as much as a glance at her companions, stepped across the threshold.

"Now, *this* is what I call *living* in a grand fashion!" Giovanni stated, remembering just in time to hold his voice down, gazing around the luxuriously furnished and tidy sitting room with avaricious eyes as he followed Libby inside.

"You can try it when you get your cut of the pot," the reddish-brunette pointed out, also studying her surroundings. "But I wouldn't come here if I was you. It doesn't strike me as being safe from thieves."

"*Thieves* couldn't do what we have," the younger twin objected with asperity, being of an anarchist persuasion despite always having lived in affluent circumstances and, because of first his parents' and then he and his sibling's well-paid acts, never gone short of any material things. Because of his political pretensions, he considered that he was engaged upon the laudable and justifiable removal of wealth from an undeserving member of the upper classes who had extracted it from the downtrodden poor. Putting aside his dislike at it being suggested that he was a thief, he continued sullenly, "Anyway, we haven't got the swag yet. I've heard they'd got a place down in the lobby that's fitted out special to hold on to their money and jewelry where it can't be reached by anybody else."

"They do have, but she told me the Countess always wants to have the jewelry where she can get at it and show it off without needing to fetch it up," Luigi growled, not any better pleased than Libby was showing herself to be over the lack of faith implied by the second part of his sibling's comment. "So all of it and any money she doesn't take with her is kept in a strongbox locked in the dressing table in her bedroom."

"If she's gone to some fancy reception, she'll be wearing all her jewelry," Giovanni grumbled.

"Not according to what she said," Luigi answered. "She reckoned the reception wasn't important enough for her to need to wear more than a few of the lesser pieces, and all the rest will be there."

"Time's wasting!" the reddish-brunette snapped. "Let's go and get whatever she's left behind."

"It's *locked*!" Giovanni stated after he had tested the double doors of the dressing table of the well-equipped bedroom into which he had followed the reddish-brunette and his brother and found was also illuminated by a lamp. "Let's see you open it."

"I could do that with a bobby pin if I had one with me," Libby declared, once again taking out the leather-wrapped set of lock picks. Selecting one, she tried it and, with some satisfaction, found it worked. While opening the doors, she went on, "There's nothing *hard* about it."

Watched by the brothers, the reddish-brunette removed the sizable wooden chest bound with steel bands, which was the most prominent thing to meet her gaze. Placing it on top of the dressing table, she had only a little difficulty before being able to unfasten and remove the padlock so she could raise the lid. Doing so brought into view the contents. Glinting in the light were a number of rings, bracelets, necklaces, pendants, and earrings, all having diamonds, emeralds, rubies, or pearls of a size that caused muted exclamations of delight from the brothers. As the collection was larger than the reports in the newspaper had suggested, even without whatever pieces the Countess was wearing at the reception, Libby was impressed by what she was seeing.

However, before any further comments could be made, the front entrance to the suite was opened and footsteps approached the dressing room.

---

1. How *the cattle business brought back prosperity to Texas is told in* GOODNIGHT'S DREAM, FROM HIDE AND HORN, SET TEXAS BACK ON HER FEET *and* THE HIDE AND TALLOW MEN.

CHAPTER TWO

STOP THE MAN!

"Go and get us a bottle of wine from the cabinet, Albert," requested a feminine voice with an attractive French accent as the footsteps came nearer to the bedroom door. "I will just make everything ready for her when she returns, then we can go to my room and share it."

From what she heard, Libby Craddock concluded that the words were being spoken by the maid of Countess Olga Simonouski, from whom Luigi Martinelli had obtained much vital information that helped her party to pull off the robbery. It was also obvious to the reddish-brunette that the fact that the French windows had been forced open had gone unnoticed, as the drapes had been left in the closed position when she and the twin brothers had come through. In spite of this, having returned from the beer garden, or wherever else she had been, the woman and the man who was with her would have to be silenced before an escape could be made with the loot.

With that point established, Libby felt grateful for another boast made by the management of the Grand Republic Hotel. They claimed with justification—and to the annoyance of the house detectives who considered it did not make carrying out their duties easier—that all the rooms were so well soundproofed, no noise from one could disturb the occupants of even the adjacent quarters. Therefore, as the new arrivals had closed the front entrance behind them on coming in, the chances of an outcry being heard nearby were greatly reduced. All that needed to be done was ensure that whatever sounds might happen were not of a volume to reach the street through the open French windows. There was no doorman on duty at that hour, but a chance passerby, or returning guest, might have heard something. If it should happen something was heard by only one person, she was confident that Jinks was capable of silencing any attempt at raising the alarm.

With the reddish-brunette, to think was to act.

Darting across the room swiftly, without waiting to see what the twins were doing, Libby flattened herself against the side of the wall behind the door that opened inward. By the time she arrived, showing she possessed knowledge of how to act in such a situation and was prepared to do so, she had drawn the knife from its sheath and held it in such a way that the six-inch-long blade could be used for either a thrust or a slash. Not until she was in position did she give her companions any attention. What she saw satisfied her that, fearing the consequences of being caught in the act of robbing a wealthy guest who probably could wield considerable influence over the local authorities, at least one of them was just as prepared to take action.

Crossing the threshold from the sitting room, the maid proved to be a pretty and shapely woman in her midtwenties. Either she had received the expensive garments and jewelry she was wearing from her mistress, or was taking the chance on wearing them without sanction. Whichever the cause might be, it was obvious she had been drinking not wisely but too well while away from the hotel. What was more, continuing to look to her rear, she was several steps beyond the door before she became aware that all was far from being well in the suite. The discovery did not come about as the result of seeing the reddish-brunette.

"Luigi!" the maid yelped, turning her gaze to the front and staring in surprise at the older of the twins. "What are you—!"

The question was brought to an end uncompleted.

"Stop the man!" Libby snapped, darting forward.

Giving the order, the reddish-brunette clapped her left hand over the maid's mouth. Pulling back on the woman's head, her arrival having been so unexpected that no resistance was offered, she used the knife in the way she considered most suitable for the occasion. Assuming her victim was probably wearing corsets to attain such pronounced hourglass contours, she had no intention of directing the weapon where it could be deflected or otherwise prevented from sinking home in a way that would have achieved her purpose. Instead, passing her right hand across the maid's shoulder, she moved the razor-sharp cutting edge of the spear-point blade so that it sank into the exposed white throat. Going deeper until the jugular vein and windpipe were severed, the slash also prevented its recipient from being able to make either an outcry or utter a scream of horror.

"What's up, Michele?" called a man from outside the bedroom, his New England accent having a suggestion that he, too, was intoxicated.

While delivering the murderous attack and hearing the question spoken in a masculine tone that was more querulous than demanding, the reddish-brunette saw that the younger twin was acting upon her instructions. However, to her annoyance, the elder was making no attempt to do anything constructive. Rather, he stood by the dressing table as if he had been turned to stone and his mouth trailed open, moving spasmodically as if trying to utter words that he could not articulate.

Showing none of the revulsion that had come to Luigi's face and frozen him into immobility, snatching out the knife he had on his belt, Giovanni dashed by the women. Going into the sitting room, he was brought face-to-face with a slender and fairly handsome young man whose attire was that of a sedentary worker in the lower wage range spending a night of enjoyment. Finding himself confronted with the menacing figure presented by the younger of the twins, the man—a valet of the housekeeping department—let out a startled and fear-filled yelp. In spite of the reaction, proving his drunken state did not prevent him from realizing he could be in deadly peril from the armed intruder, he hesitated for only a moment before turning and starting to dart toward the main entrance to the suite.

The delay proved fatal.

Before the terrified valet had taken three steps, Giovanni bounded into the air and delivered a kick to the center of his shoulder blades, which precipitated him helplessly headlong against the sturdy timbers of the door. Although the impact rendered him unconscious, it did not save him from sharing the fate of the maid. Following up the attack swiftly, the younger twin dropped until kneeling on the center of his victim's back to deliver a lethal coup de grâce in the same way Libby had finished off the maid. Ignoring the few convulsions given by the stricken valet and the blood gushing onto the thick carpet covering the floor, he straightened up and wiped the blade of his knife clean on his right thigh.

The indifference being displayed by the younger twin was not being duplicated by his sibling.

"D-d—!" Luigi croaked, as the fatally injured woman was released by the reddish-brunette and crumpled to the floor with the red of the liberated blood gushing over her less than adequately covered ample white bosom. "D-did you have to do *that*?"

"What should I have done?" Libby demanded in annoyance as she bent to clean her weapon on the bodice of her victim's gown. "Let her go out and start screaming until she woke the whole goddamned place?"

"You could have knocked her unconscious," the older twin suggested, his concern being less for the young woman than out of a realization that he was now involved in something far more serious than just a robbery. He and his brother had incurred considerable gambling debts well beyond the capacity of their legitimate earnings. Because they were being subjected to demands for early payment and threats of reprisals—from men he knew were capable of carrying them out—if the money was not forthcoming, he had been just as eager as Giovanni to accept the request for assistance made to them by the reddish-brunette. However, he had never envisaged such a situation as had arisen and, although not generally troubled by scruples, he was deeply perturbed by the consequences. "I've seen you do it before now when somebody's riled you."

"And when she came 'round, she could tell the police who you are," Libby pointed out coldly, bending to make an examination of the jewelry worn by the almost dead maid with no more display of emotion than if she was doing it by invitation. "She'd recognized you and you said you got her keen on you by telling her who and what you are. Leaving her alive knowing that much wouldn't have made good sense, would it?" Without waiting for a reply, she straightened up as she had ascertained that—expensive though they might appear at a distance—being seen from close up established that the trinkets were of no value. Concluding there was no point in taking them, she called, "Have you got the son of a bitch, Van?"

"He's not going to go nowhere, and even if he could, I've locked the door," the younger brother answered, his words drawing nearer. "And he won't be making no noise, either."

"Get ahold of yourself, Lou!" Libby commanded harshly, returning her attention to the older twin. "And start putting the stuff from the strongbox into the bags."

"I—!" Luigi began.

"Move it, damn you!" the reddish-brunette hissed, looking as dangerous as she had when launching the attack upon the maid. "The longer we're here, the more chance of the Countess coming back and, like you've figured out, we've gone way beyond just a robbery now."

"I didn't kill either—!" the older twin commenced, but stopped as he realized the intended reminder could be injudicious under the circumstances when made to the totally unscrupulous and ruthless kind of person he had always suspected the sensual-looking woman to be.

"No, but you were here with us," Libby countered, and the look that came to her beautiful face warned Luigi it had been wise of him not to finish what he had meant to say. "And that makes you just as guilty as we are, it's what is called being an accessory during the act. Besides that, I think Van would go along with me if I had to tell the police it was you who killed them both. Now move yourself, you chickenhearted bastard, so we can get clear and won't need to have to do it."

"Something wrong?" Giovanni asked, slouching into the bedroom and looking from one to the other of its living occupants.

"Your older and *supposedly* tough brother's getting tenderhearted—or being close to having the shit scared out of him—over what's happened," the reddish-brunette stated, cutting in over the words that the older twin was spluttering in Italian. "Now tell him to get the lead out of his boots so we can make our getaway. I figure doing it sometime before tomorrow morning would be nice."

"Libby's right, brother," Giovanni stated in the same language as was being instinctively used by his sibling. "We're in this game *far* too deep for you to start worrying because blood's been spilled. We have to get the money the loot will bring, or it will be *our* blood that's spilled, along with some of our bones being broken. The bastards we owe to are capable of doing both if we don't pay them by the time they gave us to do it."

The reminder of why it had been necessary for himself and his brother to agree to participate in the robbery had a steadying effect upon Luigi. Not overburdened with scruples under normal conditions—in fact having none—it had been his first contact with sudden and violent death that caused his reactions rather than experiencing any feelings of remorse for the woman he had charmed into betraying her trust so as to obtain the information required by Libby. He was also realizing that things might go badly for him if he continued to antagonize the reddish-brunette and his brother. Anybody who was as willing as she had been to take the life of another person in such a cold-blooded fashion was not to be trifled with. Nor, he fancied, would Giovanni be any less likely to respond in a violent fashion to anything that threatened to prevent the acquisition of the money they both so badly needed.

Furthermore, already the older twin was realizing that the solution to the problem of repaying the gambling debts was available and he was also aware that the need to get away from the hotel without delay was imperative. Giving a shrug, he pulled the small canvas sack from beneath his belt and joined his brother, who was already doing so with another brought for the purpose, in putting the jewelry into it. With the task completed and the neck of the sack secured by its drawstring, he fastened it securely to the back of the belt where it would not be in his way while carrying out the first and most difficult part of the departure.

"Keep watching Jinks for any sign that somebody could have seen us," Libby ordered as she and the brothers went onto the balcony. "I'll go up—!"

"Why *you* first?" Luigi asked, meaning to do no more than give a reminder that he and his brother were heavier and would be a greater strain upon the strength of Stanislaus Padoubny so they should precede the reddish-brunette.

"Don't worry," Libby answered, her tone and manner chilling. "I can't get up there and cut the rope to leave you stranded any more than you could do it to me. In either case, whichever it was would tell the police where to find the rest." Then, realizing she could be putting an idea into the heads of the brothers that might be acted upon without a thought of the consequences to the perpetrators, she went on in an equally menacing fashion, "Go ahead if that's the way you want it, but don't forget Laus and Jinks are *my* men and they wouldn't take it kind should anything happen to stop me coming after you. What's more, I'm the only one who knows where to sell the loot at a reasonable price. Besides, you're carrying *it* with you, not me."

"You go first, Libby," Giovanni offered, to his credit never having given a thought to the possibility of a double cross any more than his sibling had when posing the interrupted question. Like his brother, he did not need to be reminded where the loyalties of the other two participants in the affair lay. Therefore, he had no doubt what their response would be if anything happened to the reddish-brunette who exerted such a control over them that they gave her complete and unswerving loyalty. To do so where Padoubny—who rarely needed any faking to carry out the various feats in his act as a strong man—was concerned would be tantamount to asking for reprisals of the most painful and possible fatal kind. Nor, as past events had proven, would Jinks prove any less dangerous regardless of his physical appearance. "We've done all right so far by following what you said."

Satisfied that she had once again attained her moral ascendancy over the two brothers who had been so essential for the success of her plan, the reddish-brunette gripped the rope in both hands just above one of the knots tied to offer a more secure grip and gave a sharp tug at it. For a moment, knowing how limited the intelligence of the man above was at the best of times, she wondered whether he would have remembered the instructions he had been given and were repeated just prior to her unaided descent. Then, feeling a jerk in return and satisfied that he had not forgotten, she placed her right foot against the wall.

Bracing herself and inclining her body to the rear, the reddish-brunette started to walk upward. She was helped in this by Padoubny's exerting his enormous muscle power to draw the rope upward. In fact, after a few seconds, she realized that she could not have made the ascent regardless of her own not inconsiderable strength and agility. As it was, she was soaking with perspiration and breathing heavily by the time she arrived at the top.

"You do it?" Padoubny said, more as a statement than a question, as Libby stood on the balcony and released the rope.

"We've done it," the reddish-brunette answered breathlessly, but did not offer to mention that the affair had not gone off without blood being shed and murder being done.

"Want me to cut rope 'n' leave 'em down there?" the strong man asked. "Jinks said I should."

"No!" Libby denied, not in the least surprised that such a proposal would be made by the fifth member of their group. Jinks had developed a devious nature as a means of offsetting his lack of other qualities. However, she considered that the explanation of reasons for the refusal that she had given to the brothers might be beyond Padoubny's limited comprehension, so she made one she felt sure he would be able to appreciate. "They've got the loot with them."

"Then I better get 'em up," the strong man admitted, taking the point, albeit with reluctance. "One of 'em's pulling for me to do it."

There had been some justification for the concern that caused Luigi to ask the reddish-brunette the misunderstood question. Stating the intention of going next, which came as no surprise to his sibling as he had always been the dominant one despite being the younger, Giovanni made the climb more slowly than she did. In fact, it seemed to the older twin that he would never receive the notification. However, he eventually felt the tug indicating he was at liberty to go up. He found doing so as demanding a task as had his predecessors. Nor was this surprising, as, on reaching the balcony, he discovered the strain of drawing them up had been taking a steadily increasing toll upon even the exceptional strength of Padoubny. Like himself, the huge man was perspiring copiously, and he released the rope with a gasp of relief. It had, Luigi realized, been a very close thing that he arrived at his destination before Padoubny was unable to continue drawing him upward.

"All right!" Libby said after she and the men had regained their composure and badly depleted strength. "Get that rope up and 'round you again, Laus. Then put your clothes on. You can let me have the loot, boys. It'll attract less notice in my reticule if anybody should see us going out."

CHAPTER THREE

MY *JEWELRY*. IT'S *ALL* GONE!

"What do you think, Belle, is our good Colonel's other
guest of honor a Russian spy?"

Listening to the question put to her by Horatio A. Darren, Belle Boyd—who had won fame and the sobriquet
"Rebel Spy" for her specialized services to the Confederate
cause during the War Between the States—could not help
thinking how his attitude toward her had changed for the
better since the first time they had worked together.[1] Then,
like many other members of his gender with whom circumstances had caused her to participate on assignments
in the civil conflict and since signing the oath of allegiance
to the Union when it ended and becoming a member of
the United States Secret Service—despite having far less
experience, he had tended to treat her in a condescending
fashion.[2] Now that they were once again required to work
in cooperation, he had shown respect for her point of view
and a willingness to go along with whatever suggestions
she made, which—although she was not an overreacting
feminist vociferously claiming to be able to do everything
a man could do, and far more efficiently—she found most
refreshing.

All in all, Belle and her companion made an attractive
picture.

Particularly as there was only one other member of her sex present who came close to duplicating her physical attractions, albeit being possessed of different bodily contours, Darren was willing to concede Belle was an exceptionally fine figure of a woman. Nor, disregarding their being engaged upon the same assignment as members of the United States Secret Service, was he averse to being seen in her company. In fact, it was flattering to his ego to have noticed the way a number of the male guests were looking at him in an envious fashion.

Five feet seven in height and at the start of her late twenties, beneath what appeared to be blond hair coiffured in the latest style, the Rebel Spy had a beautiful face that its makeup could not entirely conceal with intelligence and strength of will in its lines. Supplemented by the amount of expensive-looking jewelry suitable for the occasion, the equally à la mode ball gown she was wearing showed to advantage that, while undeniably slender, she was far from being either bony or flat-chested. In fact, the moderately extreme décolleté of the garment established that her bosom was firm and quite full, but not to the point of being disproportionate for her build.

Not that Darren was without physical attraction where members of the opposite sex were concerned. Six feet tall, broad-shouldered, and trimming down at the waist, as was shown by the formal evening attire he had on, he had the build of an athlete who kept in good condition. Hard experience in his line of work, at which he had grown proficient since the first less-than-amiable meeting with Belle, his face had become more handsome now that it had acquired lines indicative of maturity.

Although neither of them was a snob or a social climber, the reception that the Rebel Spy and her fellow agent were attending was of interest to them for only one reason. Having as its host a colonel in the United States Ordnance

Department, with the exception of one person present, none of the guests would have been highly rated in the society of Washington, D.C. No officers of higher rank than his were attending, and even majors were scarce. Only a few of these had on the yellow, blue, or red collar facings indicative of belonging to the Cavalry, Infantry, or Artillery branches of the service, respectively. Of course, unless the wearer had achieved distinction in action, such men were considered of less importance in the capital city than those who wore the buff of the staff; even the black of the Medical Department were held as being higher on the scale of acceptance.

Mingled among the military men were a few minor politicians of the kind who were always on the lookout for encounters with somebody who might help forward their careers. The other civilians were either involved in the sale of weapons and hoped to benefit from showing friendship to a man who might be willing to bring favorable attention their way and lead to sales of their products, or were the owners of small businesses who were never asked to go anywhere higher up the social level.

Being a member of the Secret Service, Darren did not fall into any of those categories. He was there on the pretense of being an escort for Belle. Her presence had been arranged by the head of their Bureau under the pretense that she was Elizabeth "Betty" Hardin, granddaughter of General Jackson Baines "Ole Devil" Hardin—who had served with distinction in the Army of the Confederate States and, despite having been left confined to a wheelchair by a riding accident,[3] was now a major force in the affairs of Texas—visiting the capital for a vacation.[4] Colonel Henri Fantin had been willing to offer the invitation in the hope that doing so might cause the General to exert influence with politicians from the Lone Star State in Congress to give backing for a project upon the successful conclusion of which would provide him with an avenue to promotion. In addition to knowing what motivated her husband, Mrs. Fantin was pleased by the prospect of having a second guest under her roof who was of a higher social status than was usually the case at their functions.

The exception to the general run of the guests was Countess Olga Simonouski, and she stood out from the others—with the exception of Belle Boyd—as being the best-dressed, most voluptuous woman present. Possibly aided by the rather more than acceptable makeup she had on, as many of the other women whispered cattily among themselves, her almost classically beautiful face gave no suggestion that she was over thirty years old. Of just over middle height, the style of her piled-up raven-black hair and the high heels of the footwear that occasionally showed from beneath the flaring hem of her gown tended to make her appear taller. She was close to buxom in build, but her would-be detractors among the guests of her sex were of the opinion that her wasp-waisted hourglass contours were at least in part acquired by artificial aids. They had also been disappointed when she came in wearing only a small portion of the collection of jewelry she was reported to have brought from Russia and the pieces were of modest dimensions. The Rebel Spy had concluded that, as was the case with her own choice, the selection had been made to avoid offering a further cause for animosity among the other female guests.

From the moment the Countess arrived, to be greeted with an effusiveness equaled only by that accorded to "Betty Hardin," her behavior had been beyond reproach. Her English was good, but with a strong accent frequently punctuated by waves of a dainty brocade reticule much like the one Belle was holding. She had been, if not over-friendly, at least pleasant to all the other women before allowing herself to be approached by the men. During their brief conversation on being introduced, Belle had formed the opinion that she was being studied with the same care she herself was employing. However, after having passed a few commonplace remarks and the Countess saying she would like the opportunity to visit a ranch in Texas, but without attempting to get an invitation to go to General Hardin's OD Connected, they had parted company.

"I wouldn't like to say," the Rebel Spy admitted, in response to the question put by her companion. "If she is, there doesn't seem to be anybody or anything here she'd expect to be worth cultivating."

"That Captain Whitehead we were introduced to might be," Darren asserted, nodding to a tall young officer who walked with a slight limp, and explaining without the clarification being requested, which had been caused by a fall from a horse and resulted in his being compelled to serve with the Ordnance Department instead of remaining in the Cavalry. "He's involved with testing that new modification for the Gatling gun that the Army are taking considerable interest in."

"From what I know about the Colt Company," Belle said dryly, "they'd be only too willing to sell some of even the new improved Gatling guns to the Russian government, and there wouldn't be any need for her to attempt to find out what's happening, or try to get hold of the plans for whatever the modification might be."

"Probably you won't have heard," Darren answered, realizing his companion had just returned from an assignment in Texas and would be unlikely to have had time yet to catch up with all that was going on of interest to their organization.[5] "The British, French, and Turkish governments haven't forgotten the Crimean War yet and are putting pressure on Congress not to allow sales of arms or ammunition to Russia. And you know how wary Our Masters get when it's anything the Limeys might be able to turn into revenge for the 'Alabama Arbitration.' "

"I should," the Rebel Spy admitted, but her voice held neither bitterness nor malice as she continued. "That's what caused us to meet for the first time."

"Lord, was I *raw* in those days," Darren said, smiling wryly. Then he became serious and went on. "Anyway, she seemed to have taken quite a shine to the good captain, although I would have thought her aims would be higher if she is after the gun. We *both* know something of that sort has happened before now."

"She might consider he's sufficient for her needs," Belle pointed out, giving no sign of having heard her companion's last sentence, although she was aware of what was implied by it.[6]

"She might at that. He will have access to all the reports and other information about the trials," Darren conceded. "But even if she should get hold of plans, or even an example of the modified gun, would the Russians have the skill and facilities to make some?"

"If they don't have, they could easily find some country willing to accommodate them," Belle replied. "The Belgians, for one, are always willing to make money doing things like that."

"Then you think it is worth our keeping up with the watch on her?"

"I don't see any reason to stop."

"That wouldn't be because you like being 'Betty Hardin' and living high off the hog in the Grand Republic at the taxpayers' expense, would it?" Darren inquired.

"Would a good if reconstructed Johnny Reb like me enjoy living somewhere called the *Republic*?" the Rebel Spy countered. "And you're starting to think like your dear uncle Alden."

"Good Lord, am I?" Darren cried with well-simulated

horror. It had been the man to whom Belle referred who—despite being prissy and self-important along with other less-than-desirable qualities—was the not unsuccessful senior coordinator for the Secret Service along the middle reaches of the Mississippi River until retirement, and responsible for his enrollment as an agent. "I really must watch out against *that!*"

"WELL, good night, my dears," Countess Olga Simonouski said, favoring the young couple—with whom she had ridden from the reception to the Grand Republic Hotel in Colonel Fantin's coach from the reception, although they had not traveled out together—with a glance that implied she guessed why "Betty Hardin" had really wanted an answer in the affirmative when inviting her to join Horatio A. Darren for a nightcap. "But I have a most busy day in the morning."

Although the Rebel Spy had contrived to have their host offer transportation for the Countess, Darren, and herself when the affair at his home came to an end, she had to admit she was no nearer to finding anything to confirm or deny whether the other woman was a spy for the Russian government. Their conversation had been on a light level, with the Countess remarking at the beginning—in a manner implying she was treating somebody who did not qualify for the category by her standards as one fully conversant with such matters—how dreary she felt the couple must have regarded the whole evening. Having noticed that their reticules were somewhat similar in size, shape, and decorations, by a coincidence such as no writer of fiction would dare allow to happen in one of his works rather than deliberate selection, she had hoped to find some excuse that would allow her to "accidentally" examine the other one. No opportunity had presented itself by the time they had reached the floor upon which they had adjacent suites, and she had reconciled herself to trying to find some other means of settling the point.

Restraining an impulse to deliver a kick to the provocatively swaying derriere of the Russian woman as she went, in a manner suggestive of relief at having finally been able to leave company she considered as beneath her, toward the door of her suite, and took its key from her reticule, Belle walked onward accompanied by Darren. Before they had reached the entrance to the accommodation rented by the Rebel Spy, they heard an annoyed exclamation in Russian. Halting and looking around, they saw the Countess trying to insert the key into the hole.

"Is something wrong?" Belle asked, still deliberately refraining from using the honorific that everybody else at the reception—even Darren, much to her amusement—had employed even more often than was required by convention when addressing the aristocratically imperious black-haired woman.

"I can't get the key in," the Countess replied, always being one for stating the obvious in a way that implied she believed the explanation would not have occurred to the person to whom she was making it.

"Let me try, Countess," Darren offered, striding back swiftly.

Following her companion, Belle wondered whether the incident might be turned to their advantage in any way. She had no idea why the key would not enter the hole, but hoped Darren could change the situation; she did not wish to employ her ability in such matters, as letting it be seen was sure to arouse suspicion if the black-haired woman was a Russian spy. There was no need for the Rebel Spy to feel any concern on the point. Having experimented briefly, remarking that it seemed somebody had left another key on the inside, Darren manipulated the one he was holding until it sank in deep enough for turning it to be operative. Although Belle concluded that the Countess was clearly perturbed by what she was told could have caused her failure to effect an entry, she made no comment as the door was pushed open and she was allowed to go through.

The Rebel Spy had been correct about the way in which the Russian woman felt on hearing why her key could have failed to perform its function; she found good cause for alarm as she crossed the threshold. Taking in the gory sight of the dead man lying supine on the floor—although the worst effect of it was hidden, as he was facedown and the gaping wound in his throat was not in view—she let out a scream and could not help dropping her reticule. She was still standing rigid, frozen into horrified immobility by the discovery, when Darren stepped by her with his right hand going beneath his jacket. However, despite duplicating the surprise and repugnance she was displaying regardless of this not being his first encounter with violent death, he was sufficiently in control of himself to refrain from drawing the Remington Double Derringer he was carrying in the concealment offered by the carefully designed holster in his vest.

Following the other two into the suite, Belle, too, was momentarily taken aback by what she found. However, having been forced on many occasions to come upon such terrible sights ever since circumstances compelled her to become an agent for the Confederate States Secret Service, she recovered even more swiftly than the other two. Looking down at the corpse, she noticed the reticule dropped by the Countess and decided she would take advantage of this, as no opportunity had been offered for her to examine its contents before.

"Go fetch one of the hotel guards, B-*Betty*!" Darren ordered in a tone indicative of his tightly tensed emotions.

Before Belle could do more than feel satisfied by the

way in which her companion had retained sufficient control of himself to avoid employing her real name, the Countess gave another brief screeched-out comment in Russian and dashed across the sitting room. Instead of doing as Darren wanted, the Rebel Spy went after the black-haired woman. Entering the bedroom, the Countess gave another shriek. However, from close behind, the Rebel Spy noticed she did not devote more than a glance in passing at the corpse of the young woman—rendered even more horrific by its having fallen in a supine position that allowed the extent of the injury to be in sight—lying just inside. Instead, she dashed to the dressing table and glared into the open strongbox on its top.

"What is it?" Belle asked as the Countess began to babble something rapidly and incomprehensibly in her native tongue.

"My jewelry!" the black-haired woman replied, realizing she was not making herself understood and reverting to English. "My *jewelry*. It's *all* gone!"

"Has anything else been taken?" the Rebel Spy queried.

"Some money," the Countess answered in a surprisingly uninterested fashion and without showing any surprise at the calm way in which "Betty Hardin" was behaving. "But *that* isn't important. It's the jewelry I care about."

"Didn't you keep it in the hotel's strong room?" Belle inquired.

"Of course not," the black-haired woman denied vehemently. "I always want it where I can get whatever I need without having to wait for the box to be fetched. But we must do *something*!"

"We had," the Rebel Spy agreed. "You'd better go into the bathroom so you can't see the—this and the other while I do as Horatio said."

Nodding, the Countess walked by the corpse of her maid without doing more than giving a shudder in passing.

Following and waiting until her advice had been acted upon, being ready to claim she had made a mistake due to being so perturbed by what she had seen, Belle went to pick up the other woman's reticule. Nothing happened to indicate that what she had done was noticed by the black-haired woman, and even Darren paid no attention to it. On leaving the suite to do as she had been told, she opened the dainty little bag and looked inside.

"Well, now," the Rebel Spy said quietly as she removed and studied an object her fingers had detected beneath the material. "If you aren't using the hotel's strong room, Countess, why do you have the key for a safe-deposit box?"

---

1. *The first occasion Belle "the Rebel Spy Boyd" and Horatio A. Darren worked together on an assignment is recorded in* TO ARMS! TO ARMS! IN DIXIE!

2. *Details of the family background and special qualifications possessed by Belle Boyd are given in* APPENDIX ONE.

3. *How the riding accident was sustained by General Jackson Baines "Ole Devil" Hardin is told in* Part Three, "The Paint," THE FASTEST GUN IN TEXAS.

4. *Another occasion when Belle Boyd pretended to be Elizabeth "Betty" Hardin is recorded in* THE QUEST FOR BOWIE'S BLADE.

5. *What the assignment in Texas was is told in* THE NIGHT-HAWK.

6. *The comment made by Horatio A. Darren referred to the incident early in Belle Boyd's career described in* MISSISSIPPI RAIDER.

CHAPTER FOUR

THEY MUST HAVE CLIMBED
TO THE BALCONY

"Southrons hear your country call you," Belle Boyd said to the only other person in the small yet obviously flourishing shop she had entered.

"Up, lest death or worse befall you," Albert Higgins replied, instinctively giving the required response on hearing the words that were occasionally served to identify members of the Confederate States Secret Service to one another. As he realized what he was doing, he peered at the speaker as if shortsighted—although this was far from being the case—over the pince-nez he always wore far down his sharply pointed nose when in his place of business. Short, slender, and sharp-featured, he had always reminded his visitor of a weasel. Apart from his hair having grown thinner and turned gray, he had hardly changed since the last time they had met. Nevertheless, as recognition came, there was a genuine warmth in his voice and it still retained the suggestion of birth within the sound of Bow Bells in London regardless of all the years he had been absent from that area. "Well, bless me soul if it ain't Miss Boyd. This is a *pleasure* and a 'onor, ma'am. And can I be of service to you in any way?"

"The Grand Republic Hotel, English," the Rebel Spy

answered, knowing there was no need for a more extensive explanation.

Riding alone down in the elevator that had brought herself, Countess Olga Simonouski, and Horatio A. Darren to their floor at the hotel, the mechanism being equipped so it could be operated by a guest after the regular attendant had gone off duty for the night, Belle had examined the safe-deposit key without discovering anything to indicate from whence it had come. She had memorized the serial number on it and, arriving at the ground floor, had no difficulty in locating the house detective who was on duty.

On hearing why "Miss Hardin" had come to the lobby and sought him out, the burly and Germanic-looking man had wasted no time before accompanying her to the suite, and, clearly having expected a member of the "weaker" sex to do everything possible to avoid seeing such things, seemed surprised when she followed him inside. However, even if he had wanted to, he had not been given a chance to raise the point. His eyes took in the sight of the body on the floor, then swung to Darren. Before the man could speak, the agent held out a card identifying himself by his official rank of captain in the Provost Branch of the Adjutant General's Department. Although a couple of the house detective's colleagues had served in the Army and might have felt antagonism toward an officer belonging to that far-from-liked branch of the service, the house detective was a retired policeman who had served in Washington, D.C., for long enough to have learned that its members could be of assistance under such conditions.

Although Belle had been ready to apologize to the Countess—on the grounds of having become flustered by the horrors she had seen—if the exchange of the reticules had been discovered, the need did not arise, as its owner was still in the bathroom. Before doing anything else, the house detective—who introduced himself as Mueller—

asked Belle to return to the lobby and have the night-duty clerk on the desk summon the police. His explanation after she had taken her departure—that he thought it best to remove such a nice and well-raised young lady who was unused to seeing such horrors from such a gruesome sight—was much to Darren's concealed, albeit later expressed, amusement.

As a result of the Rebel Spy carrying out the instructions from Mueller and being asked to return to her room by the sergeant of the city's police department, who came with a patrolman in response to the series of blasts from the desk clerk's whistle, which she sensed was adding further to her companion's well-hidden, yet obvious to her, amusement, she had had to wait until after she and Darren had reported the incident to their superior that morning to discover what took place.

It said much for the rapport General Philo Handiman as head of the Secret Service—although ostensibly holding the same office in the Adjutant General's Department— had established with the local law-enforcement agency that Darren had been allowed to remain throughout the ensuing investigation. Reporting what had taken place in Belle's "understandable" absence, the description having caused a frosty grin to briefly come to the generally unemotional face of their superior and caused her to silently promise reprisals at a later date, the male agent had said that the most important items to have come to light were the facts that the door to the suite had been locked from the inside and, going by appearances, whoever had carried out the robbery and two murders gained access then left through the French windows in the sitting room, which showed signs of having been forced open externally. Going onto the balcony, even with the assistance of bull's-eye lanterns, the men had been unable to find any traces to suggest in which direction the perpetrators had made their escape. It had been decided that the gap between the balcony and its neighbors on either side was too great for this to offer a solution. Unlikely as it seemed, in consideration of the difficulties entailed due to the way the building was constructed, this meant they must have gone either up or down, and neither appeared to offer the solution.

Asked by Handiman if the Countess might have had whatever she obtained stolen from wherever it was hidden, Belle had said she doubted whether this was the case. She based the assumption upon feeling sure a woman would always give priority to checking upon the thing valued most highly under such circumstances. Therefore, unless she had had sufficient strength of will and presence of mind to pretend she was solely interested in the jewelry which was stolen, whatever she had acquired was not part of the loot. The Rebel Spy had countered the suggestion from Darren that the safe-deposit box could have been taken merely to prevent the Count from seeing something his wife didn't want him to see. She stated that what she had seen of their relationship while he was still staying at the hotel had led her to believe the Countess was by far the dominant one of the couple and would be most unlikely to care for her husband's opinion on the subject.

The moment Belle had returned to her suite, partly in the interests of making a start at the promised vengeance upon her companion, although her main reason was that she knew the task could prove of importance and what she meant to do must be carried out, she had accepted the suggestion made by the Countess that Darren should be assigned the task of discovering the location of the safe-deposit box. She pointed out that he would be helped to do this as she had committed the make and number of the key she had examined to paper. In the hope of thwarting whatever attempted retaliation she might be planning, sensing she was in something close to high dudgeon on

account of having to accept being dismissed from the
scene of the crimes on account of her being a mere "weak"
woman, Darren had suggested the safe-deposit box might
be at the Russian Embassy. The Rebel Spy had deftly
countered this by pointing out the Countess would hardly
have needed to take such a means of protecting whatever
she had acquired if she had left it there.

Looking as if butter would find great difficulty melting
in her mouth and as if her sole desire was to be helpful,
neither of which pose fooled the General or Darren, Belle
had said she would try to find out how the escape from
the hotel was carried out and who possessed the extremely
high standard of skill needed to bring it off regardless of
the means employed. Although Handiman had guessed
where she would go to seek the information, neither he
nor Darren raised the matter. The General had ruled on
assuming his post that, unless it was a matter of the
greatest urgency—as would become an established practice with most law-enforcement agencies in the not too
distant future—the way in which the intelligence was acquired by an agent would never be questioned by anybody
else in the organization.

Belle had never asked what brought Albert Higgins from
England to the United States, nor even whether he was
using his own name. He had admitted to being a criminal
and claimed to come from a street in London that was
almost so entirely inhabited by "villains" that if one happened to walk along it late in the evening, one would hear
mothers or wives seeing the male members of their families
off to "graft" by saying, even if the man in question did not
carry a cudgel or other means of defense or was unable to
use skeleton keys, "Got your stick, jemmy, and twirls?
Then off you go and have a nice tickle. I'll have something
to drink and a hot meal waiting for you when you come
home."

Despite finding the story amusing, all the Rebel Spy had needed to know was that, although a successful house-breaker—and especially adept in the variety performed by a so-called cat burglar or second-story man in the United States, although he had always referred to it as being "on the climb"—and safecracker in those days, he had donated his specialized services to the Confederate States Secret Service. Furthermore, in addition to having taught her much that was to be of the greatest use throughout her career with that organization, he had willingly given her support upon the assignment to which Darren had jokingly referred the previous evening.

With the War Between the States at an end, having been successful in keeping his activities against their best interests unknown to the Federal authorities, he had taken up the occupation of locksmith as a cover for his main occupation. Because the opportunities for acquiring worth-while loot were better in the North than in the South, which was kept impoverished by Reconstruction, he had gravitated there. Settling in Washington, D.C., as offering the best chances for obtaining information of use and find-ing a steady flow of victims among the numerous people of means who came there for one purpose or another, he had opened a business in the trade at which he was so expert. It had prospered to such an extent that he had, or so he always insisted to Belle on their infrequent meetings, practically given up crime as a means of earning his live-lihood. However, he still retained his numerous contacts and was in the know about much of the illegal activity that happened throughout the capital city and elsewhere in the East.

Because of the nature of her business with Higgins, the Rebel Spy had decided against going to interview him as "Betty Hardin." Instead, having all she needed for the transformation in her suite at the hotel, she had transformed herself into what appeared to be the kind of maid who came as attendants to wealthy female guests. Although she made no alterations to her face, other than leaving off the makeup worn as her alter ego, the clothing she donned and her demeanor were so different that she had walked by the Countess in the passage—giving a quick curtsy as she went by, as she had seen genuine servants do—without drawing more than a cursory and uninterested glance.

Using the servants' stairs to reach the ground floor, as was required of one of her supposed social status, Belle had become involved in a situation she would rather have avoided and yet proved to be of use later. There had been some of the housekeeping staff descending behind her, and just as she arrived on the ground floor, one—a dark-faced and Gallic-looking young man who was obviously all too conscious of his masculine charms—directed a lascivious leer at his companions and speeded up his advance until close enough to goose her. It was not, as anybody who knew the Rebel Spy could have warned, the wisest move to make against her even when she was playing a role. As soon as the hand left her rump, she had propelled her right elbow to the rear with all the force her slender yet superbly muscled body was capable of producing. Struck in the solar plexus, the man had gone reeling backward to alight sitting and winded on the lower steps. Nor had she allowed the lesson to end there.

Pivoting around, although like many of her garments it was made so it could be discarded hurriedly in an emergency, Belle had refrained from making use of the facility and had instead only drawn up her skirt to a level that allowed her to send her left leg up with the same speed she had used to deliver the blow. The toe of her footwear—a high-heeled and sharp-toed black boot into which were tucked the legs of snugly fitting matching riding breeches, although this was not discernible—passed in front of the man's face so close that it almost grazed his nose. Giving a warning that such a thing must never be done to her again as the foot returned to the ground, she had turned and walked away. Because her assailant remained seated with his mouth trailing open, she went uninterrupted and to the accompaniment of laughter and compliments—from the female onlookers, most of whom had been subjected to similar treatment, in particular.

Knowing she could do so without appearing out of character, as genuine maids were frequently accorded the same privilege when doing errands for their employers, the Rebel Spy had hailed a cab from the rank near the hotel and was transported by it to her destination.

"It would've been a nice one with a good tickle by all accounts if they hadn't made it a topping job by killing them two," Higgins had stated, knowing what was meant by the name of the hotel. "I 'aven't 'eard much, so what happened?"

"Well, English, how was it done?" Belle asked after she had answered the question. Guessing that "tickle" referred to the amount of the loot and "topping job" meant that the two murders had turned the robbery into a capital offense for which hanging would be the punishment, she had had no need to request an explanation. Instead, she gave all the information she had acquired. She did not forget to include the significant summation supplied by the hotel's doctor—who was summoned and showed what might have been surprising perception if he had not said he served in the Medical Department of the United States Army during the War and had had considerable experience where such matters were concerned—that the shed blood and condition of the bodies suggested they had been killed almost simultaneously. What was more, he had found nothing to indicate either had been allowed to struggle before the death blow with a knife in each case was inflicted. "The only door into the suite was locked and the key still on the inside, and everything else points to them having come through from the balcony from the French windows, both of which you and I know aren't too difficult to arrange."

"That it's not," the Englishman agreed. "Only, from what I know about the way things are done at the Republic, getting up to the suite wouldn't be easy by the stairs, much less riding the elevator. I don't see whoever done it hanging around fixing the French windows or the front door when they were taking stoppo, especially after what they'd done."

"I agree with you that there had to be more than one of them involved," Belle asserted, even though Higgins had not stated the point in so many words.

"I can't see them even getting to the floor without the hotel guards spotting them," the Rebel Spy claimed. "Unless they had inside help."

"They'd've needed to be a bloody sight luckier than m— anybody I know—if they managed to find somebody they could straighten to look the other way while they was going through. It's been tried more than once and never come off."

"Then they must have climbed to the balcony."

"Where's this 'ere suite at?"

"On the front and second floor."

"Then it wasn't from the ground, if there's more than one in on it, and I'd say there 'as to be," Higgins assessed. "That just couldn't be done even from the sides or the back. I know, it's been thought of and given up by some fellers who're as good as I used to be on the climb. Not that there's *many* of 'em around, and certainly not working mobbed up nor even in twos."

"Are you saying it couldn't be done, even though it was?" Belle inquired.

"I'm saying there's not more'n two over 'ere's could've done it," the Englishman corrected. "And neither of 'em's working around town."

"Only *two*?" the Rebel Spy queried.

"I'm surprised there's even that bleeding many," Higgins declared. "It's mostly all running around wiv guns waving 'n' masks over the face, or blowing things up wiv 'igh hexplosives over here, no finny-essy like what the Frogs say at all."

"From what I've heard, the Countess's jewelry was worth a great deal of money," Belle said. "Couldn't somebody have come over from Europe who has the finesse to pull it off?"

"If anybody that *good* had come over, I'd've 'eard abart it," the locksmith declared with conviction in his voice. "Do you know what I reckon, Miss Boyd?"

"I've always been willing to listen to your opinion on anything like this, English," Belle said truthfully.

"Whoever done it must've found some way to sneak in," Higgins explained, showing he was pleased by the compliment from one for whom he had developed a great respect and considered to have been his most promising pupil when giving her instruction in the finer points of committing a burglary. "Then they got up onto the balcony 'rahnd the roof and come dahn from there."

"Would doing that be easy?"

"Sneaking in would be the heasiest part, and that'd be bloody 'ard, if you'll pardon my French."

"Could they have climbed down using ropes?" Belle suggested.

"They'd 'ave to be bloody good to do it going down," Higgins estimated. "And even better than good to climb back again. That'd need something like a bleeding miracle, or a better-trained team than I've ever 'eard of. 'Course, there's allus new 'n's coming up, but anybody *that* good would soon get talked abart. I tell you, Miss Boyd, 'ow it was done's a bleeding mystery, and 'appen you solve it, I'd be obliged if you'd tell me 'ow it was done. I'd like to shake the 'ands of the team what did it, 'cepting I don't like what they did to them two poor bleeders—and one of 'em a real pretty young woman—who must've walked in on 'em."

"I know how you feel, English," Belle admitted grimly. "Damn it, I've done some things I'm not proud of in my time in the line of duty and expect to have to again, but what they did was nothing but cold-blooded and deliberate murder. I don't particularly care for the Countess, but I aim to bring whoever they were to justice if I can."

"Do you know, Miss Boyd," Higgins said pensively, "the more I think about it, the surer I get that they wasn't professional villains what done it."

"You mean that they could have been amateurs on their first robbery?" the Rebel Spy asked.

"That'd explain why I've never heard of 'em," the Englishman pointed out. "The only thing I can't work out is what kind of blokes could've done it."

"Or me," Belle admitted, realizing the amount of skill that would have been required to make the descent from the roof to the balcony on the second floor and then climb back.

Knowing better than to ask the names of the two men whom Higgins considered capable of climbing to the Countess's suite, as he had always refused to divulge such information on the grounds that he "wasn't no bleedin' nark," Belle thanked him for his help. They chatted for a few minutes about old times and mutual acquaintances from those days, then she took her departure. Absorbed in thoughts engendered by the conversation while going in search of transportation back to the hotel, she paid no attention to a large and glaringly printed poster attached to the wall of a building, although she might have drawn some significance from it if she had done so.

CIRCUS MAXIMUS PROUDLY PRESENTS
FOR ONE WEEK ONLY IN YOUR FAIR CITY
THE PREMIER ATTRACTIONS OF THE WORLD
SEE
THE GREAT ZOLTAN ASCEND IN HIS BALLOON
CAPTAIN FEARLESS AND HIS FEROCIOUS LIONS AND TIGERS
THE LOMBARDO BROTHERS, MASTERS OF THE HIGH TRAPEZE
GORGO THE GIGANTIC, STRONGEST MAN IN THE WORLD
PRINCESS MAGDALENE, KNIFE THROWER AND QUICK-CHANGE
ARTIST
JINKS THE MASTER CLOWN AND HIS COMICAL COHORTS
AND NUMEROUS OTHER ACTS TO ENTERTAIN AND THRILL YOU

According to the date and other details given in smaller print, the circus was due to leave Washington, D.C., for a tour of the Kansas railroad towns and points west in three days' time.

CHAPTER FIVE

DON'T TRY TO PULL THAT OLD GAME ON *ME!*

"Good afternoon," Libby Craddock greeted. "Are you Lachlan Lachlan of the McLachlans, like it says on the door?"

On reaching the balcony around the roof of the Grand Republic Hotel, the young woman and her associates had concealed the items used to bring off the robbery beneath garb in which they had traveled from the Circus Maximus. Then they had contrived to make their escape from the premises with no greater difficulty than was experienced on arriving and ascending to the roof. Collecting the other member of the party from where he had remained on watch in the street, they had returned to their temporary accommodation without attracting any unwanted attention.

The reddish-brunette was now about to try to dispose of the loot.

Looking at the man who she had been informed by an acquaintance with criminal connection was the best chance of making the kind of deal she wanted, Libby was far too experienced to let herself be deterred by outer appearances. There was nothing impressive about the building in which she had been informed he could be located. Nor was his business accommodation suggestive of the kind of money she intended to demand for the jewelry she had helped to steal. It was composed of two offices, on the door of each being inscribed in white paint badly in need of renewing, "LACHLAN LACHLAN OF THE MCLACHLANS, Dealer In Antiques And Objets D'Art." On one was the further information, "PRIVATE! Absolutely No Admittance" and the other bore the words "RECEPTION, KNOCK AND ENTER."

Going through the second door after having complied with the first part of the instructions, the reddish-brunette had found herself in a small and grubby office that smelled of stale cigar smoke. She had been confronted by a small and wizened man with shifty pale-blue eyes in a face suggestive of a less-than-honest nature and which reminded her of dishonest jockeys she had known. On hearing her say she had been sent by Mr. Alastair McAdam of Glasgow, the password she was given by her associate, he had placed the thick and cheap cigar he was smoking in a stone tray holding the remains of several more and a pile of ash, which accounted for the less-than-pleasant aroma of his surroundings. Having gone through a door into the adjacent office, he had returned a few seconds later to say she could enter.

If Libby had found the other room unimpressive, she considered the one into which she had been directed was little better. Nothing about its furnishings—an ancient desk, a couple of chairs from which the stuffing was protruding, a stove in which a fire was burning regardless of the day being warm, and a scuttle filled with coal alongside it—or wall decorations implied that she was in the presence of the man her acquaintance had claimed was the most affluent fence for stolen property anywhere in the United States.

Rising from the chair at the opposite side of the desk to where the reddish-brunette was coming, as the door through which she was admitted was closed behind her to leave them alone, the man looked her over with the same interest she was devoting to him. There was, she decided, something theatrical about him. Just under six feet tall, he was almost skeletally lean and gaunt in build. His sharp, pallid features had the texture of old parchment and seemed just as lifeless in texture. They were not rendered any more pleasant by a pair of beady black eyes and a somewhat large hooked nose. Nor was his appearance improved by being topped with what her trained eyes detected was a wig of longish white hair. Finally, he was clad in far from expensive or new somber black attire that put her in mind of that worn by a "doom and damnation"–threatening circuit-riding preacher belonging to one of the lesser and stricter religious denominations.

For his part, the man seemed to find his visitor just as unprepossessing. That was, she realized, her own fault. Putting to use the ability learned from her father and exploited in the second part of her billing as "Princess Magdalene, Knife Thrower and Quick-Change Artist"—the poster advertising the Circus Maximus did not mention that she was also "Chieftainess Swift Eagle of the Mohawk Nation, Equestrian Marvel," "Lady Lavina, Escapologist *Nonpareil*," and "Daring Donna, Trick Shot Extraordinaire," and in each capacity she was sufficiently proficient as to perform adequately when aided by judicious trickery for some of them, on various occasions—she had made sufficient changes to her appearance to feel sure he would be unable to recognize her if they met at some later date.

Sufficient of the wig Libby had on was deliberately made to straggle from beneath a grubby white spoon-bonnet to show it was an eye-catching red hue. By wearing horn-rimmed spectacles with darkened lenses, having added a most realistic if unflattering false nose, and with two of her front teeth blackened out, she had removed all traces of voluptuous attractiveness from her face. Including the much-worn buffalo-hide muff on her right hand and equally ancient-looking bulky brown bag in her left—in a black glove that concealed all trace of her marital status— her clothing was no better than would be worn by any woman in the lowish-rent district to which she had come. What was more, while the achievement was no mean feat, it was designed to prevent all signs of her body's shapely feminine contours from showing. To complete the disguise, she walked without any of the seductive grace she could adopt when called for.

"That is my name," the man admitted after a moment during which he and his visitor had scrutinized one another. His voice had a burr almost as pronounced as that used by entertainers seeking to establish that their origins are in Scotland. "And you, my clerk Beagle tells me, are a friend of Mr. Alastair McDonald of Glasgow, my old home-town and that of my clan."

"His name's 'McAdam,' as you know damned well," Libby answered with a timber that was unidentifiable by any regional or local accent and totally unlike her usual sensually promising tone, or the more threatening one she adopted when annoyed by something. "So let's forget being cagey and get down to business."

"Before one talks business," Lachlan answered, sinking onto the chair he had risen from with seeming reluctance when the reddish-brunette entered and waving to her from the opposite side of the desk, "one always prefers to know who one is doing it with."

"If I told you my name was Mrs. Katey Smith," Libby answered as she placed the bag on the scuffed top of the ancient desk but did not remove the muff, "I'd bet you the best pork dinner in town, if you go for that sort of grub, you wouldn't believe me. And you'd be right not to, al-though I'm not going to tell you what it really is, so let's get down to what's brought me here."

"I frequently eat pork, although I'm not interested in betting," Lachlan said coldly. "Now, who are y—!"

"Are *these* introduction enough?" the reddish-brunette interrupted and tipped some of the loot acquired in the previous night's robbery from the bag.

"Are they what I think they are?" the fence asked, staring with all-too-obvious interest at the pieces of jewelry that lay before him.

"They are," Libby confirmed. "And the rest of the swag's in here. Do you want to look it over and make me an offer, or sit swapping lies about our names and where we come from?"

"You are not what you seem, I suspect, *Mrs. Katey Smith*," the fence challenged.

"No more than you are, *Mr. Lachlan Lachlan of the McLachlans*," the reddish-brunette countered in a similarly mocking tone. "So let's not start asking about *true* names and get down to business, or I'm walking straight out of here. You aren't the only fence I can take them to."

"What you've shown me is called being in possession of stolen property by the law," Lachlan stated in a threatening fashion, and there was a slight bump as he laid his right forearm on top of the desk.

"And the law is the *last* thing you want coming here," Libby pointed out. "So what is it to be, talk a deal or I go elsewhere?"

"I can't talk business until after I've examined the merchandise to decide upon its value," the fence warned, accepting that he was dealing with the gang of amateurs he—like Albert Higgins, unbeknownst to him—had deduced, from what he had already heard about the robbery at the Grand Republic Hotel, had carried it out and did not know how to handle the sale of the loot.

"Then examine to your heart's content," the reddish-brunette authorized calmly, tipping the remainder of the jewelry into view still without removing her other hand from its place of concealment.

Staring not without a certain amount of avarice showing at the glittering mound before him, Lachlan used his left hand to extract a jeweler's lupe from the top drawer of his desk. However, he used both as he began to subject each piece in turn to it in a way that indicated to Libby he knew full well what he was doing, not that she had doubted such would prove the case. As he went on with the scrutiny, he frequently emitted grunts redolent of disappointment or uninterest and set aside one of the larger pieces. By the time he had concluded the lengthy and thorough examination, they were in the majority and were kept separate from the lesser pile of smaller items.

"Well?" Libby prompted when a few seconds had elapsed without her receiving a comment of any kind.

"I don't want to disappoint you, Mrs. Katey Smith, after the excellent piece of work you and your gang did last night," Lachlan responded, contriving to sound more dourly Scottish than before as he gestured with his left hand at the smaller pile. "But *this* is all that's of the slightest interest to me. All the rest are nothing but costume jewelry Countess Simonouski fetches with her to impress people, and I'll bet the real stuff is back in Russia safe and sound somewhere. Genuine pieces that good are kept in either a vault at a bank or, in this case, the strong room at the Grand Republic."

"Is that so?" the reddish-brunette asked, keeping any expression of how she felt over what she had been told from showing on her disguised features.

"You can believe me," the fence asserted, his voice redolent with what passed as complete conviction. Taking a stack of well-used bank notes from the drawer that had yielded the lupe, he started to count some of them out while continuing, "But there, I can see you weren't trying to put something over on me and it was all nothing more than a mistake on your part. Such often happens on one's first job. Anyway, I don't mind losing a few bucks against the time you come up with something really worthwhile, so here's what I'm willing to do."

"Is that *all* you're willing to offer?" Libby inquired after she had been quoted a far-from-munificent price for the smaller pile of jewelry.

"It's even a bit more than they're worth," Lachlan claimed with what seemed like sincerity. "The way they were got, they're so hot it'll be a long time before I dare try to get rid of them. And the same applies to the rest of it. Here, I'll show you exactly what *they're* worth."

While speaking, the fence began to scoop up as much of the larger pile as he could hold in his two cupped hands. Crossing to and deftly opening the lid of the stove with his foot, he tossed the jewelry inside. Remembering what had happened on previous occasions when he had behaved in such a fashion, he had expected some response from the woman at his desk. Yet he heard nothing. What was more, on turning around, he could see no indication on her face or in her attitude to suggest she was alarmed, or even surprised, by what he had done. Rather, her face had a cold and grim expression that did not change as he walked across to gather up the remainder of the pile.

"Don't try to pull that old game on *me!*" Libby commanded in the most harsh and menacing tone she could produce. "It's just about the most ancient fence's trick in history. I know a few minutes in a slow coal fire doesn't harm good stones like they all are in the least, and, as you'll have them taken out of their settings then melt down the gold from them, it won't be too damaged to be salable."

"Is that so," Lachlan said quietly, and dropped his right arm to his side. "Don't try anything rash, Mrs. Katey Smith. This room is soundproof, except for in the office next door, and I can rely upon Beagle's discretion and assistance in *anything* I need doing."

"Mine's *bigger* than yours!" the reddish-brunette warned, bringing her right hand into view from the muff for the first time. "And, if I need it, I can kill you, then do the same to that man of yours when he comes in here."

Even as the fence was pressing the inside of his forearm against his jacket to cause the spring-loaded mechanism of the device resembling the card hold-out employed by some gamblers to activate and put the Remington Double Derringer it held out of his sleeve, he discovered its presence had either been detected or suspected by his visitor. On making the comment, she had produced a pearl-handled and fancily decorated nickel-plated Smith & Wesson No. 3 American revolver with a six-inch-long barrel and was pointing its muzzle—which seemed much larger than its .44-caliber to him under the circumstances—in a disconcertingly steady fashion directly at the center of his chest. Although the double-action mechanism precluded the need, the hammer was drawn back as an aid to even more rapid discharge, with a reduction in the chance that the lesser trigger pressure required would have an adverse effect upon the aim.

Although neither of the office's occupants realized it, the weapon could have supplied a clue to Libby's true identity. It was one of the matched pair she had had converted, including having the rifling grooves of the barrels removed to allow her to use shot instead of a single solid bullet, for use when she was being "Daring Donna, Trick Shot Extraordinaire," at the circus. However, the hold-out never having failed to produce the desired effect before, Lachlan was so disconcerted to find that his own—as he had believed unsuspected—weapon was countered before it could even be aligned to pay that much attention to the one with which he was being covered.

"Not that you can count on that runt in there," Libby continued, after giving a piercing whistle without allowing her gun to waver away from its aiming point. It was followed immediately by a yelp of alarm from Beagle and a quick scuffling sound. "I've a man with him who's big and strong enough to break him and you in half if I give the word. So put that stingy gun on the desk and go fetch the jewelry out of the stove. When that's done, we're going to talk *real* business without any more arseholing around, and you might as well get it into your head right now that I know for *sure* how much they're worth at fence's prices. So don't try to offer me a thin dime less after what you tried to pull."

"Do you know something, Mrs. Katey Smith?" Lachlan said after the deal was concluded and a sum that met with his visitor's satisfaction had disappeared into her bulky bag. He had had time to think while doing so and draw the previously unnoticed conclusion from her physical appearance and the weapon she handled with competent skill. "I can use somebody with your talents if you are what I feel sure you'd have to be, the way you took the Grand Republic."

"And what do you feel sure I am?" the reddish-brunette inquired, halting instead of carrying out her intention to leave now that the deal was concluded in a way she desired.

"One of the people from the circus that's in town," the fence replied. "And so are the rest of your gang. You're leaving for the West in three days, aren't you?"

"We are," Libby admitted, neither confirming nor denying the supposition.

"By train?"

"Yes, we're having a special for the whole show."

"Do you and your gang have to travel with it?"

"We're not forced to. Why?"

"Because if you go by the main westbound two days from now instead," Lachlan said with a quiet, serious demeanor that was impressive, "I can put you in the way of making some money that will be far more than you've just taken from me."

CHAPTER SIX

BAD LUCK, COUNTESS

"We all liked what you did to Frenchie," a perky-faced and dainty hotel maid with an attractive Southern accent told Belle Boyd as they met on the stairs leading to the second floor of the Grand Republic Hotel as she was making for her suite. "He's been asking for it for a long time, him and his wandering hands."

"And I won't miss with the kick if he tries anything like it again," the Rebel Spy stated with a smile. "You can tell him that from me if you're so minded."

"That's real *good* of you-all, and I'll do it first time I see him!" the Southern maid enthused, then looked harder at Belle and went on. "Hey, I don't remember seeing you around here before—what did you say your name is?"

On her return from visiting Albert Higgins, without taking the time to change from the disguise she had adopted for doing so, the Rebel Spy had reported to General Philo Handiman what she had learned. He had said he would pass on what she told him, without of course disclosing the source from which it came, to the detective lieutenant of the Washington, D.C., Police Department assigned to the case. He had been successful in fending off suggestions from the Bureau of Foreign Affairs—passed to him through the usual channels employed to prevent his more important capacity from becoming too widely known—that his organization should take over the investigation of the crime, despite its already being in the hands of the civic authorities, as a means of assuaging possible complaints from the Russian government over what had happened to one of its extremely wealthy nationals while visiting the United States.

After commenting that she was pleased that her superior had been able to prevent their department from being given extra work, on learning that Horatio A. Darren had not checked in from searching for the safe-deposit box to which the number of the key she had obtained belonged, Belle had said she would resume being "Betty Hardin," then go and try to help locate it. However, arriving at the Grand Republic Hotel, she was still attired in a manner that would not allow her to go to the second floor in the elevator. Taking the servants' stairs, she had met the Southern maid and a question she had hoped to avoid was directed at her.

"I only got here this morning," the Rebel Spy lied, having said her name was "Daisy" and being told to call the young woman she was addressing "Dixie." "The agency sent me to work for Miss Hardin, and she told me to do an errand for her."

"What's she like to work for, Daisy?" the hotel maid inquired, as she would to any other servant she met.

"I think she's the nicest lady I've ever took on with," Belle claimed without hesitation, and although she spoke so as to be able to tell Darren about how highly she regarded her alter ego later, the words paid an immediate dividend. "I don't think she's ever had a maid afore and, well, you know how it is working for one like that."

"I do, and you're *lucky!*" the genuine maid declared vehemently. "The Old Hag put me in for that foreign Count-

ess or whatever she is. You know, I shouldn't say this with
her dead 'n' all, but I bet that li'l ole Froggie gal Michele
as was murdered last night would think she'd had a mer-
ciful release getting away from Her high-toned High-Up-
Iness."

"She's a bit of a slave driver, then, huh?" the Rebel Spy
inquired, considering a comment of that sort would be expected from her.

"A bit's only halfway there, Daisy, if that close," Dixie
answered. "She's had me on the go ever since I got to her,
and nothing's ever done right enough for her. I bet she'll
say it's my fault if the cab she said for me to have the
doorman get waiting for her in three-quarters of an hour's
not there right on time."

"Then I'd best let you get to doing it," Belle asserted.
"And I want to let Miss Hardin know I'm back."

Parting from Dixie with a promise that they would try
to get together for a night out later, the Rebel Spy hurried
to her suite. Once there, she swiftly removed the attire
suitable for a maid and, retaining the black blouse, riding
breeches, and boots she had on instead of conventional
underwear, she selected a specially adapted outfit she felt
sure Countess Olga Simonouski had not seen "Betty Hardin" wearing. With the garments on, she added an ele-
gantly coiffured wig of a red color suggestive of having been
acquired through the use of henna and a style different
from the blond one in which her alter ego always appeared.

Keeping her eye on the wall clock, she next applied
makeup to her face in a way that implied doing so was not
a usual event. Satisfied with the difference she created,
feeling thankful—and not for the first time—for having
received an assignment allowing her to bring along a variety
of items with which to alter her appearance, Belle collected a small and garishly embroidered reticule and a

dainty-looking tightly rolled parasol that clashed with the rest of her costume.

With everything ready, including a sum of money that she hoped would prove sufficient for her needs in the reticule, the Rebel Spy went to open the front door of the suite just wide enough to let her keep an unnoticeable watch on the passage from the gap. Her wait was not protracted to any great extent. Having been transferred to fresh accommodation, fortunately still on the same floor, the Countess emerged from it and walked in the direction of the elevator. On reaching it, she glanced around as the Rebel Spy came out of the suite and turned her way.

"Well, 'bye now, you-all, Betty honey!" Belle called in a strident voice to which she contrived to apply the accent of a Texan with less education and upbringing than the girl she was supposedly addressing. "I'm dashing off to spend some of that *lovely* money pappy gets for his cattle on buying up a whole swatch of fancy jewelry like your'n to go with these high-toned duds I've got on."

Entering the elevator before its attendant could close the doors, Belle had behaved as she felt was correct for the kind of person she was portraying by trying to engage the Countess in conversation. Watching carefully, she could detect no suggestion that the Russian woman had pierced her disguise and derived not a little satisfaction over the way in which her attempts to be "friendly" were received. Failing to have an opportunity to do more than inject a grudging "yes" or "no" into the flow of comments about life in such "a big and fancy city," the Countess was obviously relieved when they reached the ground floor and she could emerge to hurry through the main entrance. On reaching the sidewalk, she discovered that—having come to be aware of her impatience and bad temper when things went wrong—the doorman had a cabriolet waiting. Helping her inside, knowing better than to expect the gratuity most people availing themselves of the service presented, he stood back with a less-than-amiable expression on his rugged face.

"Hey, mister!" Belle said, coming from the hotel as the vehicle carrying the Russian woman was moving off.

"Yes, ma'am?" the doorman queried, noticing that the "redhead" had taken a five-dollar bill from her reticule and held it forward.

"Get me one of them fancy buggies real *fast!*" the Rebel Spy instructed, deciding against saying "pronto"—although it would have been in keeping with the persona she was creating—because it might not be understood. "That painted foreign hussy's been making sheep's eyes at my wealthy pappy and's headed to meet up with him now. I'm a-headed after her to make good 'n' sure she don't try to have her wicked ways with him."

One problem that Belle had envisaged about leaving the hotel looking as she did had failed to materialize. Although she had noticed the desk clerk and one of the house detectives glancing at her in the way they did everybody who went by, they had decided she was there on justifiable grounds—probably to meet a guest—and made no attempt to stop her for questioning. Nor did the doorman offer to make any inquiries. Instead, having deftly pocketed the bill—a larger sum than usually came his way so early in the day and for so simple a service—he had signaled to another cabriolet before the explanation was concluded. Climbing aboard and repeating her reason for what she wanted to do, along with the promise of a sizable tip if successful in keeping the other "buggy" in view without its occupant knowing, she was carried off at a reasonable pace.

While traveling along and watching her request being carried out to her satisfaction, the Rebel Spy thought impishly of what whoever in the department of the Secret Service that monitored all aspects of its expenditure was checking the list of expenses she had incurred would say when he reached the item "Riding in cabriolet—" and the sum she intended to hand over at the successful conclusion of the journey. It was more than the mere cost of hiring the vehicle would warrant, and the bureaucrats without whom no government organization was permitted to function were noted for having a penny-pinching outlook that would have shamed the stereotype the supposedly parsimonious Scot pretended to be.

After traveling for a short time, Belle found that the cabriolet was brought to a stop. Looking a short distance ahead, she discovered that the vehicle they had followed was halted in front of the First National Bank and its occupant was descending. Directing a knowing wink her way, the driver informed her that he reckoned she would not want to be too close in case the "foreign woman" should notice her and avoid going to the rendezvous with "her pappy." Agreeing that the suggestion was correct, she handed the man ten dollars to ensure the bureaucrats had something to complain about when they heard of this. Just as surely, General Handiman would insist the full amount she claimed be refunded, even though he would probably chide her in an amused fashion over her extravagance.

While moving forward, noticing that the cabriolet did not move away after the Countess emerged, Belle was ready to pretend to be looking into whichever window she was passing if the other should glance her way. Then the Rebel Spy saw a young man dressed after the fashion of a junior teller or something similar in the area coming from the bank. As he was approaching the Russian woman, having stiffened and paused for a moment as if receiving a surprise, he swept off his derby hat in a gesture closer to shielding his bespectacled face than merely doffing it to her. Nor, Belle realized when the Countess had gone by and the hat was replaced, was the impression she had formed regarding the gesture incorrect.

"Why howdy, you-all," the Rebel Spy said after advancing until close enough for the words to reach the ears of the man. "I just bet you're a real good friend of my good friend, Betty Hardin."

"Well, I'll be damned!" Horatio A. Darren exclaimed, staring at Belle.

"I don't doubt *that* in the least," the Rebel Spy replied in her normal voice. "If it's not an answer improper for a li'l ole Southron gal like me to hear, what brings you here?"

"The same as you, most likely," the male Secret Service agent answered. "Trying to find a safe-deposit box with the number you gave us."

"And you think it could be in *there*?" Belle asked in tones that implied she considered the contingency remote and noted the lens of the spectacles were made of plain glass.

"I don't just *think*," Darren asserted. "I *know* it is!"

"It's nice to know," the Rebel Spy drawled, with a well-simulated suggestion of cynicism. "So now we'll have to wait and see whether my expenses for coming by a cab were justified."

"The moneymen will query them no matter how little and justified they might strike us as being," Darren said dryly, yet successfully conveying the impression of being indifferent as he was not directly concerned. "You'll just have to hope something worthwhile comes of this."

"Now *that* is what I call a piece of greatly deserved luck," Belle stated after about five minutes. She and Darren were now seated in a cabriolet—which he had collected and kept waiting for the purpose—and were now watching the Countess coming from the front entrance to the bank carrying a black-leather document case with a coat of arms in gold on its front.

"Nonsense," the male secret agent denied in an apparently sober fashion as the statement was made. He continued in a mock modest tone, "It was all achieved by the three P's—perseverance, persistence, and plodding attention to detail. And by the kind of coincidence you'd never believe if you read it in one of Ned Buntline's books—having been in the same fraternity at college as one of the clerks. We Alpha Beta Kappa sworn brothers in blood are always willing to help one another, particularly when one is able to get the other an introduction to a lady of the theater upon whom he wished to devote his—he assures me—honorable intentions."

"I'll believe you, although many wouldn't," the Rebel Spy declared when the vehicle was set into motion at her orders. "You *can* keep your promise to your friend, can't you?"

"One has one's connections," Darren declared, oozing false modesty. "But, knowing our luck, all she's got are some indiscreet letters she wants to get rid of before her husband finds them."

"She's not going to the Grand Republic to do the destroying," Belle pointed out. "If that is all there is to it."

"Or the Russian Embassy," Darren supplemented, knowing the layout of the city better than his companion. "Which I'm relieved about if she should have something about the new-model Gatling's modification, or the way to get hold of one, in the case. We wouldn't have a chance of getting whatever it might be out of there."

"I'll go with you on that," the Rebel Spy admitted, and started to tell what she had learned from Higgins.

"Hmm, looks like she's there," Darren exclaimed before the explanation was completed. "Although it's the last place I would have expected her to be going."

"It doesn't look so bad a place she wouldn't deign to call in," Belle remarked, studying the front of Hoffmeister's

Hauf Brau and noticing that it was in a most respectable part of the city.

"It's not," Darren confirmed. "In fact, I'd go there myself if I could pay the tab on expenses. But she'll be more likely to meet Germans than Russians here."

"I'd say she seems to be expected," the Rebel Spy estimated, watching through the window as a fat and Germanic man dressed in a better fashion than the waiters was taking the Countess through a door at the rear. "Shall we go in?"

"We may as well," Darren agreed, having removed the spectacles as being no longer necessary. However, glancing at his garments, he went on, "Only, I don't look like what a customer for a place like this is known to be."

"Then it's right lucky you-all're with a rich li'l ole Texas gal who'll pick up the tab for you," Belle replied. "Only, we've got to try to see where she's gone and who she's meeting. Do you know what's back there?"

"Sure," Darren replied. "Some private dining rooms."

"Then we'll just have to make out like we want to use one," the Rebel Spy stated. "Come on, as my good friend Dusty Fog says, let's get her done."[1]

"By all means," Darren agreed, and took out money to pay the driver.

"Me 'n' my sweetie here wants to use one of them fancy back rooms of your'n I've heard tell of so much 'round the Grand Republic Hotel, which's where I'm staying while in town," Belle informed the burly man who had shown the Countess from the main dining area on entering the Hauf Brau, waving a handful of currency.

"Don't waste our time, Otto!" Darren barked when the maître de began what was intended as a refusal. He produced an official-looking card with his photographs on it and alleging he was a captain in the Provost Marshal's Department and continued, "That woman who just went in the back's a known confidence trickster and wanted for rooking one of our generals. So, unless you want more trouble than your bosses will stand for, you'd best let me and this lady operative of the Pinkerton's go to her."

"Very well," Otto Dieterle said sullenly. "But I don't think the Col—*gentleman* she has come to meet will be any too pleased."

"I'll take a chance on that and see there's no comeback for *you*," Darren promised. "Let's go and get her done, Miss Smith."

"You might at least have made me a 'Smythe' for shame," Belle said sotto voce as she and her companion went through the door into the appropriate rear portion of the restaurant. " '*Smith*' indeed."

Even while speaking, on entering a wide passage the Rebel Spy and Darren found that, with one exception, all the doors on either side were open to show small and intimate-looking rooms. What was more, they were not alone. Two large men with close-cropped blond hair and a Teutonic cast of features was standing almost at attention on either side of the closed door. Despite being in plain clothes of a quality suggesting they were not paying customers, they had the bearing frequently acquired by German soldiers, especially those of one particular part of that country.

"What you want?" demanded the taller of the men in an accent giving further support to his place of origin. "We told him in there *nobody* was allowed to enter."

"Could be he's hard of hearing," Darren replied, although he did not know how he could enforce his will upon the pair and felt sure no display of his supposed status would suffice to do so. "But we have to see in that room."

"And you *can't* do it!" claimed the shorter man, which still made him larger than the male agent.

Watching the pair moving forward, Darren wished he were carrying a revolver with which to make them halt.

But the matter was resolved before there was a need for any form of masculine action to be taken.

Sending her left hand to its specially adapted waistband, Belle caused it to open and the skirt slid rapidly downwards. Coming to a halt, the two burly man watched its descent with a lascivious interest. However, what came into view was not any kind of feminine undergarments. Instead, they found themselves gazing without comprehension at the riding breeches and boots that came into view. Nor was either granted an opportunity to recover from the surprise.

Gliding forward while her left hand joined the right on the parasol and subjected it to a twisting motion, the slender young woman sent her right leg upward in a swift yet clearly power-packed kind of kick only the very skilled exponent of *savate* she had become before commencing her career as a spy could have employed. Passing between the thighs of the taller man with the same kind of precision employed when she was dealing with "Frenchie" at the hotel—except this time she did not make it miss—the toe of her boot took him full in the base of his trousers. Such was the potent effect of the attack upon the most vulnerable portion of his masculine anatomy, he was sent back a couple of paces and, with hands clasping at the stricken area, collapsed to his knees.

Nor was the second man any better able to avoid what befell him. Already surprised by the unexpected turn of events, his discipline-dulled wits were unable to keep pace with what followed. Nor was the equally startled Darren any better able to realize what was taking place, it happened with such rapidity. The parasol held by the Rebel Spy came into two portions and, knowing what kind of person she was up against, she did not hesitate in taking steps to halt the threat he posed. Swinging the handle segment around in a slightly upward arc, she caused its concealed secret to come into play. Sliding out, a steel ball on a telescoping coil spring whipped around to strike the man at the side of the jaw. There was a crack of breaking bone and he crumpled across his retching, helpless companion like a rag doll from which the stuffing had suddenly been removed.

"I've heard about your *savate* and *that*!" Darren gasped, staring from the men to the dismembered parasol as if unable to believe the evidence of his eyes. "Now I see everything about them both was true."

"I've always found it pays to be prepared," Belle answered, stepping forward and thrusting open the door. As she stepped across the threshold closely followed by her companion, she took in the sight awaiting them and said, "Bad luck, Countess. We've caught you being a *very* naughty lady."

"What the—!" snarled a militarily smart-dressed, big cropped-haired man, whose hard features bore the dueling scars *de rigueur* with members of his class in Germany, starting to rise from where he was sharing the table with the Russian woman. Although startled into employing his native tongue, he went on in accent-free English. "And what the devil are you doing?"

"Coming to take those documents back where they belong, Colonel von Diegelmann," Darren answered, recognizing the speaker as the senior military attaché at the German Embassy, a man suspected of running its Secret Service organization.

"And I'd advise you to give them up peacefully," Belle went on, bringing a Remington Double Derringer from where it had been concealed in the lower segment of the parasol. "I doubt whether your government would approve of your being accused of buying them knowing they must have been stolen. And as for you, Countess, I don't think Colonel Riabouchinska will be enamored of your trying to sell them instead of turning them over to him. I've heard he's had people sent to Siberia for less."

A look of horror came to the beautiful yet suddenly haggard face of the Russian woman. All her hopes of acquiring a sufficient sum of money to pay off some heavy and pressing gambling debts had come to nothing. What was more, she was all too aware of the power wielded by the man named by Belle and how he had had members of the aristocracy placed far higher than herself sent into exile or worse. Therefore, she did not feel the slender woman she still failed to recognize as "Betty Hardin" was exaggerating what her fate would be when word of her attempted betrayal reached his ears.

---

1. *The association between Belle Boyd and Captain Dustine Edward Marsden "Dusty" Fog before and after his distinguished service with the Texas Light Cavalry in the War Between the States is explained in APPENDIX ONE.*

CHAPTER SEVEN

STICK 'EM UP, GENTS!

"The Countess was *most* cooperative after Colonel von Die-gelmann left in what my poppa always used to call high dudgeon," Belle Boyd reported to General Philo Handiman about two hours after she and Horatio A. Darren had returned from their productive visit to the private dining room at Hoffmeister's Hauf Brau.

"In what way?" the head of the United States Secret Service inquired, his almost always seemingly bland face giving not the slightest suggestion of how he was receiving the information. "And *why?*"

"I felt sure—!" the Rebel Spy began.

"*We* both felt sure, sir!" Darren put in quickly, having allowed the beautiful Southron girl to do the talking so far and knowing she was seeking to take full responsibility if the decision did not meet with official approval, not merely trying to claim all the credit for the successful conclusion of their assignment.

"I stand corrected, Rache," Belle drawled, using the abbreviation of her fellow agent's given name for the first time in their acquaintance and, despite the gravity of the situation, humorously comparing him with an earlier associate with the same sobriquet.[1] "*We* decided official policy would prefer the matter not to be made public. So on our promising not to have any legal action taken against her provided she told us the name of the man who provided her with the copy of the documents she was going to sell—and went to join her husband on his hunting expedition—she was only too eager to oblige."

"I'm pleased young Whitehead wasn't the one," Handiman said after having heard the name of the man responsible. "His father is a friend of mine of long standing, and he's had a rough enough time, being permanently seconded away from the Cavalry because of his injury."

"Yes, sir," the Rebel Spy agreed, concluding that what she had just heard was yet another example of the humanity that always lay beneath the seemingly uncompromising exterior of her superior. "She only played up to Captain Whitehead to help divert attention from her man if it was found out he'd copied all the information. The trouble is, even if *their* policy would want it kept out of public notice, going by what I know of the system, doing anything to the goddamned bureaucrat who pulled the deal with her will be practically impossible."

"It always is when one of them betrays his trust," Handiman concurred.

As was the case with the way in which much of the United States was organized, despite having split away from Great—as it was then—Britain back in 1776, Congress had adopted the system that their former parent country used—what it termed "civil servants," a means of ensuring a continuance of running for the government, albeit from behind the scenes, when the sway of electoral results brought about a change of the political parties in office. Because of the power that was given to the bureaucrats, as was—and still is—the case in England, it rendered them practically immune from punishment even when, as was the case under discussion, one was willing to make the most of his, or later her, position of trust by betraying it.

"There isn't anything we can do about von Diegelmann either," Darren said, showing annoyance.

"And no reason why we should if there was," Handiman stated firmly. "He was only doing his duty, and what I'd have expected any of you to do under similar circumstances. I'll send him an unofficial apology for what happened to his men."

"Then we can say the assignment is over, sir?" Belle asked, displaying what appeared to be convincing innocence as her superior turned a quick glance redolent of understanding, if not entirely approving of how she had gained entrance to the dining room, in her direction.

"It is, except for one unofficial thing," Handiman replied, and having explained what it was, went on. "You're both on furlough for an indefinite period effective upon leaving this office, and *officially* unofficially I don't want to know where you can be found, even if it should be at the Grand Republic Hotel, Miss Boyd, Mr. Darren, although I don't know what Accounts are going to say when they get the bill for the two of you staying there."

"Thank you, sir," the Rebel Spy replied, pleased by the latest example of her superior's generosity and regarding it as a sign of his approbation for a task well done, but deciding against mentioning the comments that would greet the amount of money she had put down on her expenses for the cabriolet she had used to follow Countess Olga Simonouski.

"STICK 'em up, gents!"

Seeing who had uttered the words in a high-pitched boyish treble, neither Charlton Forbes nor Archibald Fine felt concern for their safety or property.

Despite being aware of the importance of the mission

they were carrying out, even though they were traveling
without the usual escort provided in the interests of avoiding attracting unwanted attention their way, neither of the
pair considered their latest assignment on behalf of the
Treasury Department to be anywhere nearly so potentially
dangerous as others they had undertaken successfully.

Not only were the Treasury agents satisfied that the way
in which they were transporting a set of plates for printing
currency to a new mint that was to be opened in San
Francisco was a carefully kept secret, they were more than
pleased with the means by which it had been arranged for
them to make the journey. As would be the case when
they reached the transcontinental railroad at Chicago, they
were traveling through the first night of the trip in a luxurious private car and had attire and a suitable expense
account to give credence to the pose of being wealthy men
headed for California on business. There was nothing to
suggest their charge was in a seemingly innocuous suitcase
resting on the baggage rack. Yet each was highly skilled at
his work and very competent with the Colt Storekeeper
Model Peacemaker revolver in a spring-retention shoulder
holster concealed beneath his jacket.

Looking at the speaker as he was advancing toward
them, the agents were sufficiently at ease that they cheerfully complied with the words he had spoken. Not much
over four feet six, he was clad in the kind of attire pur-
porting to be that of a cowboy, which was much favored
by boys of the age he gave the impression of being. Although there had been no sign of his parents' being nearby,
the men had seen him at the depot dressed in the same
way and with a bandanna drawn up in the fashion of a
mask, which prevented all of his features below the wide-
brimmed and high-crowned hat from being discernible.
While there, he had repeatedly approached and pretended
to menace people with a toy revolver fitted with a rolled

strip of paper holding small detonating charges of the kind once used to avoid the need to fit a single percussion cap to a firearm before each successive shot could be fired. On being fired to enforce the "demand," it gave off a sharp crack but was otherwise completely harmless.

"Don't shoot, mister!" Forbes requested in what seemed to be a pleading tone.

"By cracky, Charlie," the other agent boomed jovially. "It must be that desperate outlaw, Jesse James!"

"You're *wrong!*" the masked figure stated, but the tone of his voice had taken on the timber of a much older person than he appeared to be.

Even as the intruder was speaking, Fine began to grow aware that something was different about his appearance.

Just an instant too late, as a similar feeling was beginning to assail his companion, the agent realized what was wrong.

Instead of the thing pointed toward the two men being a harmless toy, it was a short-barreled Webley's Bulldog Model revolver.

Before either agent could recover sufficiently from his surprise and take defensive measures for his protection, the already cocked weapon crashed and sent a .44 Webley–caliber bullet between Fine's eyes. Then, deftly using the recoil kick as a means to cocking the action once more with his thumb in a way that implied he possessed strength beyond what might have been expected for one of his diminutive size, the masked figure turned the barrel and fired again. Swiftly though the move was made, the second piece of lead plowed into Forbes's left breast and brought his belated attempt to arm himself to an immediate halt.

Showing either a lack of precaution or evidence of faith in his ability with the gun, the masked figure returned it to the holster on his gunbelt. Then, turning, he hurried over to lock the door through which he had gained admittance—it having imprudently been left unfastened so a waiter could bring food and drinks from the club car—and went to ensure that the one at the other end was also secured. Having done so, he went to draw down a window as far as it would go and leaned over to wave several times while looking upward.

Receiving the awaited signal from below, Giovanni Martinelli and Stanilaus Padoubny sank until lying facedown on the roof of the private car, and splayed their feet apart for added support as they made ready to carry out the instructions they had received. With the younger twin lying across his sibling's thighs and rump to give further assistance in what they all—even the massive professional strong man—knew would be a demanding task, the other two contrived to lower Libby Craddock by the wrists over the side of the compartment. Like them, she was dressed in the attire used during the descent from the roof to carry out the robbery at the Grand Republic Hotel.

Having heard what Lachlan Lachlan of the McLachlans wanted her to do and the maximum price he claimed his principals—he had stressed that he was merely acting as a go-between for them, which she had believed, and not unexpectedly declined to supply their identities—were willing to pay, the reddish-brunette had said she would give it her consideration. Based upon what he had told her about the way in which the printing plates were to be transported to California, taking into account the specialized services of two of her companions in particular, she had come up with what she had considered to be the solution most likely to succeed.

Libby had decided that putting the scheme into effect on the first night of the journey would be the wisest course, as it was unlikely the escort for the loot would be expecting anything of the sort to happen so soon after leaving Washington, D.C. On being told something of what was planned, but not how the robbery was to be carried out, the fence had stated his approval of the time she had chosen on the grounds that it would allow him to put the loot into the hands of his principals without undue delay. He had not suspected that, even though she had demanded and received an advance payment, she had no intention of parting with such a valuable commodity in the way he envisaged.

In accordance with the plan concocted by the reddish-brunette, after the smallest of her associates had sought to establish he was carrying a harmless toy cap pistol at the depot, they had boarded the train separately and clad in attire that gave no suggestion of their connection with the Circus Maximus. In fact, she had been disguised as a woman whose face was concealed by the veil of her black "widow's weeds" garments. When satisfied it could be done safely, the brothers having heard the escort ordering a meal and drinks from the club car's attendant at nine-thirty and saying they would leave open the door of their compartment so he could deliver it, which had simplified matters, they had gathered outside the car. Removing and concealing their outer attire while their diminutive companion waited ready to play his part, they had climbed onto the roof of the car to await his signal that all was ready for the scheme to continue.

Being lowered as far as the men holding her could manage, the reddish-brunette required assistance to enter the private car. However, she had taken this into account when laying her plans. Still leaning out, the small masked figure quickly wrapped his arms around her legs. Then, displaying an even greater indication of his strength than when handling the heavy and powerfully kicking Webley, he drew her inward until she was able to signal for her wrists to be released and arrived inside the car without more than a minor difficulty.

"Good work, Jinks," Libby praised somewhat breathlessly, for the descent had put a considerable strain on her and, for all her confidence in Giovanni and Padoubny's ability to do what was required, she was relieved it had been accomplished with such comparative ease. "Did you have any trouble?"

"None," the diminutive figure replied, drawing down the bandanna to bring into view the tanned and not bad-looking features, except for the shifty glint in his pale-blue eyes, of a man in his mid-thirties. "It went off just like you said it would. Not that I thought it wouldn't, unlike *some* I could name."

"Don't let that worry you," the reddish-brunette said reassuringly, crossing to the baggage rack and lifting down the first of the suitcases from it. "Our Italian friends and Laus have just about finished their usefulness, and the time will soon be on hand for them to retire *permanently*."

"I'll kind of miss that big stupid lummox. He had his uses providing no brains were needed," said the man who was billed by the Circus Maximus as "Jinks The Master Clown" and never mentioned his actual name. "But not the wops. It's a pity we couldn't have left them behind, dead of course, at the Grand Republic."

"It couldn't have been done, more's the pity," Libby answered. The set of skeleton keys from the pouch on her belt and skill at picking locks allowed her to open the suitcase, and an examination proved its contents to be just clothing. "Still, everything comes to those who wait."

"Only don't let's wait too long," Jinks requested.

"I won't," the reddish-brunette promised, taking down another case. On opening it with no more difficulty than she had experienced with its predecessor, she gave a low hiss of satisfaction. "*This* is what I'm after."

Removing the heavy oilskin-wrapped bundle that aroused the comment, Libby placed it into a drawstring-necked sack from underneath her belt. However, as she was about to turn, an idea struck her and, saying she might as well see if the men had anything else of value, she opened and scrutinized the contents of the remaining baggage. Despite failing to locate anything of value, some instinct caused her to turn out all the contents and subject the interior of the cases to an equally close examination. Beginning to gaze even more intently at the lining of the last, she let out another sound indicative of satisfaction and drew the knife from its sheath.

"I was right, Jinks!" Libby breathed after she had slit open the lining and removed another set of almost identical lead printing plates. "The bastards were playing it cagey. We'll check over both sets and work out which of them are genuine when the circus catches up with us. Right now, we'll get back to *them* and go down to get dressed in something suitable for us to be seen. Are you still going to be all right in that crate?"

"Yes," Jinks replied. He had been put aboard the caboose of the train in a large locked wooden box that had airholes bored along the upper sides and was claimed to be housing the reddish-brunette's pet Pekingese. "Only, you'd better have the conductor tell whoever's been kicking the side to stop it. I'm getting tired of having to bark like a dog each time it happens."

---

1. *Information regarding the connection between Belle Boyd and the earlier "Rache" is given in* RENEGADE.

1a. *The "Rache" in question makes a "guest" appearance in* MCGRAW'S INHERITANCE.

CHAPTER EIGHT

THERE'S SOMETHING *FAMILIAR* ABOUT THE ROBBERY

"That was a *very* short furlough, even for this department, sir," Belle Boyd said dryly as she entered the office of General Philo Handiman, although she and Horatio A. Darren—who had met her in the passage—knew the matter that brought them there must be of some urgency.

What was more, the Rebel Spy and the male agent had already unknowingly reached the same conclusion over why they had been summoned to meet the superior in the United States Secret Service.

"Accounts said the taxpayers shouldn't keep on being burdened by the expense of keeping you in a place as costly as the Grand Republic Hotel, Miss Boyd," the General replied, instead of getting down to business immediately after the social amenities he only rarely overlooked were observed. He made the comment in such an apparently somber tone, he might have been serious rather than ironic. "And they are just as adamant that you ought to be in less extravagant accommodation than you have at present, Mr. Darren, as *they* are paying for it."

"Somebody somewhere must love Accounts," the male agent sighed in a seemingly heartfelt manner. "But I'm damned if I know who they might be."

"You've seen the account in the newspapers this morning?" Handiman said, more as a statement than a question.

"I did order a most delightfully high-priced breakfast in my suite, which I mean to put down with my other expenses," Belle confirmed, knowing to which item in the morning's newspapers her superior was referring.

"Along with the ten dollars you've already claimed for the cab ride you took," the General said in a mock-disapproving tone, as Darren was signifying concurrence with the Rebel Spy.

Although there was no longer any need to do so, the subject of her attentions having taken the advice she had given before they parted at Hoffmeister's Hauf Brau, Belle had retained the suite taken for her to enable the surveillance of Countess Olga Simonouski to be simplified, reveling in a luxury far greater than she usually was granted when on an assignment. Darren had stayed in the less palatial accommodation he had used. Not that either was allowed to remain in relaxation for long. Each had anticipated the arrival of the note, delivered by a mounted messenger who showed signs of having traveled at some speed, ordering them to report to headquarters as soon as convenient, which both had known meant straightaway whether convenient or not.

"What's behind the story of the robbery on the train, sir?" Darren asked.

"I'm pleased that the *Washington Mail* have handled it just as one would have expected of them," Handiman declared after having told all he knew about the incident. "It simplifies things for us, although I'm sure that was never the editor's intention when he included it."

The comment aroused chuckles of appreciation from the two agents, despite each being aware of the situation's gravity and why the head of their organization was taking such an interest as he implied they were to become involved.

Although not the largest of the newspapers published in Washington, D.C., the *Mail* was of a distinctly liberal persuasion, which led it to always seek out—even fabricate on occasion—any items detrimental to the government, the military, and the forces of law and order. While its competitors merely reported that two guards were killed while pretending to deliver printing plates for currency to a new mint opening in San Francisco, the *Mail*—which normally would not have regarded the murder of men following such an occupation as being worth mentioning—demanded to know why they were deliberately sacrificed in such an unnecessary fashion.

"Do you know, sir," Belle said, "there's something familiar about the robbery."

"Such as?" Handiman prompted.

"The way the doors of the private car were locked with the keys left on the inside and one of the windows was open, for starters," the Rebel Spy obliged. "As it must have happened earlier at night, doing that wouldn't have been so easy as it would in the Grand Republic."

"That's true," the General admitted. "The waiter who delivered the meal, then discovered the bodies when he had the conductor open up, offered a reasonably close estimation of when it happened. The trouble is finding out *how* it took place."

"Like why a pair as smart and well used to such things as Charlie Forbes and Archie Fine let somebody get close enough to shoot them down without either being able to get his gun clear," Darren suggested, having met the two men in the line of duty and retained their friendship. "There aren't many they would trust. In fact, I'll bet they told the waiter to make sure it was him and nobody else who fetched along their order. Which being the case, they wouldn't have sat still if a stranger came with something pretending to be what they'd asked for."

"They might have let a woman get close," Belle offered. "That's how the Bad Bunch down in Texas got away with it for so long."[1]

"Knowing what they were carrying, even if it was only fake plates," Darren answered, "I don't believe they would have let a woman come as close as from where they were shot while on the job."

"Or a priest, like Beguinage used to pretend to be?" the Rebel Spy asked, referring to a hired killer, claimed to be the most deadly and successful in Europe, who had come to Texas to carry out an assignment.[2]

"Neither was a Catholic," the male agent replied. "Or religious enough to let a preacher of any other kind, or even a nun, get near enough to do it without one or the other of them fetching out his gun. They might not be as fast as I've heard Dusty Fog and some of those other Texans you know so well are, Belle, but they weren't exactly slow either."

"Well, it happened, no matter how it was done," Handiman asserted. Then there was a knock on his door, and as a booming voice sounded from the passage without the words being discernible, he went on, "Ah, it sounds like the man I've asked to come and meet you has arrived."

There was something theatrical about the appearance of the tall and well-built man who entered the office upon the General's calling for him to do so. Fairly handsome in a florid fashion, with bushy eyebrows and an equally auburn mustache of sizable dimensions, his features expressed a bonhomie and his deep-set dark eyes twinkled with amusement as he strode as if leading a parade of the more garish kind rather than merely walked forward. He carried a broad-brimmed black hat, and a black cloak lined with red silk hung over the shoulders of his stylishly cut dark suit. A multihued cravat was secured to the frilly bosom of his white shirt by a stickpin with a large ruby. His step was jaunty, and other than that he was well past the first flush of youth, nothing about him gave any suggestion of what his actual age might be.

"Hello, Barnie, you old reprobate," Handiman greeted, rising and shaking hands with the visitor. "What's your latest attraction, another Ki-Chu?"

"No more of *them*, thank you," the visitor boomed in a voice that was clearly used to making itself heard over considerable distances. "Dash it all, Philo, the last one I had got religion in Boston, Mass., of all places. Right in the middle of my introduction, with his cage surrounded by assorted gilpins and rubes all agog over me expounding how he was a tailless Ki-Chu, the monkey that looks so much like a man that no attorney-at-law dare go near his cage for fear people would think the Ki-Chu had escaped when he pulled off his wig and false whiskers, then told them I, me, Phineas Taylor Barnum, with all undue modesty the *Greatest* Showman On Earth, was nothing but a fake. Such a display of base ingratitude cut me to the quick, wherever *that* may be, I may tell you."[3]

"I can see how that could be somewhat embarrassing," the General declared without any show of sympathy. "Now let me present you to my two young friends. This is Miss Belle Boyd, and, before you ask her, I'm ordering her to tell you of her own free will that she *doesn't* want you to lead her to fame and fortune equaling that of Lavinia and Tom Thumb."

"Egad, that is a *pity!*" Phineas T. Barnum boomed, eyeing the slender girl with open approval and admiration. "I can visualize it all now. Dressed in a suitable fashion, you could demonstrate how you most justifiably became known as the Rebel Spy, my dear lady. Why, I might even be able to get the almost equally famous Scout of the Cumberland to engage you in a recreation of the great battle of fisticuffs in which you and she engaged at a theater the name of which escapes me for the nonce."

"There's only one slight trouble with that," Belle replied, her demeanor showing amusement. "I never even met Pauline Cushman, much less engaged her in a bout of fisticuffs, as you put it."[4]

"The latter is of little import, dear lady," the showman claimed with the grandiloquence of manner that was second nature to him. "The gilpins and rubes believe it took place, and I consider there is something most meritorious about fulfilling their desire to see a belief brought to fruition."

"I truly admire a man who thinks so much of others," Handiman said dryly, and introduced Darren.

"And now, Philo," Barnum said, taking the seat that was offered after having shaken hands with the two agents. "How can I be of assistance to you?"

"What do you know about the Circus Maximus?" the General asked.

"Old Cosmo Cathneiss's little show?" Barnum intoned as if the mention of the name was close to being anathema where he was concerned. "They've just recently been gracing your fair metropolis with their presence, if that is the correct word."

"It will do until something better comes along," Handiman declared.

"*We* aren't due to play here for some time," Barnum said, making the words have the implication that he felt his small audience—and the population of Washington, D.C., in general—would be the losers because of the absence. "But it has gone down considerably of late. The balloon Cosmo goes up in isn't a bad attraction, especially when he has it turned loose instead of being moored to the ground. The cats in the act are so old they couldn't chew milksop, much less their trainer, or *he* wouldn't be in with them. Although Momma and Poppa Martinelli were good in their day, those sons of theirs aren't more than passable. Cosmo's strong man is all right. Nothing spectacular, but not much needing to be faked. That little feller Dinks is a good clown, and he's more proportionately formed than many of them. One of his games is to get dressed up as a cowboy bandit, with a bandanna over his face, and pretend to hold folks in the crowd up with a toy cap pistol that sends out a flag with 'Bang' on it when he pulls the trigger." Giving no sign of noticing the way all three other occupants of the room stiffened as they heard the last words, he went on, "But he's no Tom Thumb, and has a temper that makes most of us shy away from hiring him."

"How about the women I saw mentioned on the bills?" the General queried.

"There's only one of them," Barnum stated. "Except for a few overage flashers who can't do more than walk around the ring to make it look like there're more of them working than is the case."

"Just *one* woman does all those acts?"

"Just the one, Philo, although she doesn't do them all every night, regardless of what Cosmo implies. Her name's Libby Craddock, and she's better than fair at everything she does. Whatever might be lacking, she covers it up by having quite a physique that she shows off most satisfactorily by the way she's costumed for the part she's playing."

"If she's that good," Handiman said, "why haven't you or one of the other big shows picked her up before now?"

"For the same reason Jinks is still with Cosmo," Barnum explained. "Only even more so. She's such a good shot with a pistol that she blew the ba—made the ringmaster of one show so he wouldn't hope ever to raise any children when he tried to molest her. Which nobody could blame her for, as she wasn't the first he'd done it to, even though some thought it a trifle extreme. Then, in another show, she laid open the face of a Gypsy girl who ran a mitt camp— fortune-telling concession to you gilp—with a knife quicker than a flash when they both fancied the same man. There have been other incidents of a like nature, and these combined to make owners shy away from taking her on."

"Do you happen to have a poster for the circus, sir?" Belle inquired, just beating Darren to speaking and equally amused as the men by the way in which the visitor had only just refrained from referring to them as 'gilpins.'

"I have," the General confirmed, and came to his feet.

"Does the escapologist act she performs entail picking locks, Mr. Barnum?" the Rebel Spy wanted to know, after her superior had collected the poster from where it was standing in a roll alongside a filing cabinet and spread it open before her.

"That it does," the showman agreed, nodding as if to indicate he believed a shrewd point was being made. "And very good she is at it, by all accounts. In fact, I've heard there were a couple of times money was found missing from locked cash boxes. There was some suspicion on account of her known skill, but her own nature and having Jinks and Padoubny the strong man backing her play, nobody got around to trying to prove it."

"So the three of them have been together and close friends for some time?" the Rebel Spy said quietly.

"They have indeed," Barnum substantiated. "I don't know what she sees in them, but, according to what I've heard, they would do anything for her without question."

"You wouldn't know whether there have been any unexplained robberies take place where they were appearing, sir?" Darren said, showing he was duplicating Belle's line of thought.

"I'm afraid not," the showman replied.

"Damn it!" the male agent exclaimed. "I've always said it's a pity there isn't a central collecting agency where lawmen could send information like that to be available to others when needed."

"I've tried to have one set up up several times," Handiman claimed. "But I was always turned down by Our Masters, as I think you call them, Rache, because of the expense setting it up would entail and fears that the liberrad softshells would object on the grounds that doing so would entail a loss of privacy for everybody who was kept on the records."

"Before you ask," Barnum said, and for once his voice lost its usual timbre. "Yes, I think Libby and her two friends could have pulled off the robbery at the Grand Republic with the help of the Martinellis. Climbing up and down the wall would be possible even for her, with Padoubny hauling in the rope on the way back."

"How about the way the train was robbed?" Belle asked.

"I'd say they could have pulled that from the roof of the private car," the showman assessed. "But not so the guards missed seeing them coming in."

"Unless the killing was done before the others got in through the window that had been opened for them," Handiman pointed out, despite having nodded as if approving of the theory being propounded by the Rebel Spy.

"That could have been done by Jinks wearing his masked-bandit outfit," Darren asserted. "You said Charlie and Archie were shot by heavy-caliber bullets that stopped either from cutting loose in return after they were hit, sir. Knowing how experienced they were, I don't see them mistaking any kind of gun that was large enough to take one— even a Remington Double Derringer, which would be about the biggest he could handle if he's so small—for a harmless cap pistol."

"He wouldn't need to use the Remington, because of

his size," Barnum warned. "He's as strong as many men a whole lot bigger, and I heard he once shot a drunken horse-wrangler from out west who tried to pick on him with his own Colt Peacemaker."

"Only, even a Civilian Model Peacemaker would be too big to be passed off as a cap pistol," Darren objected.

"A Storekeeper Model might get by, especially as it would be expected when they thought they were just watching a child playing a game of outlaws, which is how Jinks must have looked to them," Belle pointed out, knowing that the major difference between the two types of Colts lay in the one she mentioned having a two-and-a-half-inch barrel against the other's being four and a three-quarters in length. "And there are others on the market of a large enough caliber that are just as compact."

"That's true," Handiman agreed. "The circus left by train going west this morning, so—!"

"Libby and her bunch weren't with it," the showman interrupted. "I had one of my men at the depot to see them off and learn where they'd be playing so our routes wouldn't clash and, I'll admit, trying to find out whether Cosmo had come up with any new attractions I might be able to persuade him to let join up with me. He asked about her specifically, as they'd been on good terms once and he's still got a shine on her, and was told they'd gone ahead on the train that got robbed, only that wasn't mentioned outright."

"Would they all be in cahoots?" Belle inquired.

"I'd say not," Barnum estimated. "It was before the newspapers came out, so they wouldn't have heard about the robbery."

"Then they could have done both of them," Darren stated.

"They *could*," the General admitted. "The only problem will be proving what we suspect." Seeing that the showman was exhibiting signs of wishing to leave, he asked, "Is there anything more you can tell us, Barnie?"

"Only that you don't want to take chances with *any* of them if what you're thinking proves correct," Barnum replied soberly. "Because even the two wops—Giovanni especially—could prove real dangerous given the opportunity to resist, and there's no *could* about the rest."

"What's next, sir?" Darren inquired when the showman had taken his departure after having told Belle that he wished he could persuade her to go against her orders and take up his offer of appearing with his organization. "Was it really a just a decoy scheme thought up by the Treasury Department that went wrong and got Charlie and Archie killed, like the *Mail* says?"

"It *wasn't*," the General replied, speaking in what was a most definite manner to anybody who knew him as well as did his two agents. "But we're going to do everything we can to make the gang and whoever's behind them think it was. Because I'm sure they had to have somebody with more facilities than they're likely to have let them know where to look and when to do it. What we have to do is convince them the *real* plates are going to be sent to San Francisco by a roundabout route and a courier nobody would be likely to suspect the Treasury of using and, because of interdepartmental rivalry, we aren't going to be allowed to become involved."

"It's a pity we dealt with that bureaucrat of the Countess's the way we did, Belle," Darren remarked. "Fed the right news, I bet he'd soon find where to peddle it to the best advantage even if he didn't already know."

"And it's lucky he isn't the only bureaucrat willing to do things like that," the General remarked in a casual-seeming fashion. "We've got one on tap who we've let sell items we wanted various people to know about without knowing he's been set up to do it."

"Then we'll have to hope he can convince them that it will be me taking the supposed real plates while somebody else is doing it, sir," Belle guessed.

"If there's one thing I've never been able to stand, it's a smart woman," Handiman declared. "I married one and know just how smart they can be."

---

1. *Information about the murderous gang of outlaws to whom Belle Boyd refers is given in* THE BAD BUNCH.

2. *What happened when the European professional killer came to Texas is told in* TEXAS ASSASSIN *and* BEGUINAGE IS DEAD.

3. *How another American entrepreneur sought for a living example of the same kind of mythical creature is told in Chapter IX, "The Ki-Chu,"* BOSAMBO OF THE RIVER, *by Edgar Wallace.*

4. *Details about one incident in the life of Pauline "the Scout of the Cumberland" Cushman, a spy for the United States Secret Service during the Civil War, is told in Chapter Four, "The Major,"* THE TEXAN.

CHAPTER NINE

IT'S *ME*, OR THE LAW

"Wha—!" Lachlan Lachlan of the McLachlans gasped, starting to rise with his right hand going toward the uppermost drawer of his dilapidated desk as he saw that the person who had entered his private office unannounced was not the one he expected and remembered that the Remington Double Derringer in its card hold-out holster had failed to achieve the expected surprise when he last tried to use it. "Wha— How—?"

"That crooked hardboot you call a clerk's gone to the john, so I let myself in," Libby Craddock explained as she gazed without favor around the grubby room in which she had last conducted her meeting with the scrawny fence. She was dressed and looked as she had been then. Gesturing with the bulky bag she was carrying in her left hand and slipping the right inside, she went on. "I must say you don't seem very pleased to see me."

"I never thought I would!" Lachlan admitted, being too disconcerted to wonder how his far-from-welcome visitor had deduced that Beagle was a jockey who had been warned off for dishonest behavior—carried out at his behest—as he started to slowly and, he hoped, with an appearance of innocent intent, ease the drawer open.

"Leave the damned thing in there, you stupid son of a bitch!" the reddish-brunette ordered viciously, bringing the fancy-looking pearl-handled Smith & Wesson revolver, which she could handle in a deadly fashion when need be, from the bag. "I thought you'd have learned better than to play games with me after the last time you tried, and I sure as hell don't know why you're at it again, unless you're hoping to get them without paying."

After having contrived to return Jinks to the prepared box in the caboose without being detected by the conductor or anybody else, Libby had found that the rest of the gang were just as successful in reaching the seats they had chosen on boarding to lessen the chance of it being realized they were traveling together. The discovery of the corpses had happened earlier than she envisaged. In fact, she had been surprised that it had happened so quickly until she had learned why the door to the private car was left open. However, while there was the considerable commotion she had known was certain to take place under the circumstances, nothing had occurred to make her believe she or any of her companions were suspected of being responsible for the killing of the two Treasury Department guards and robbery of the currency printing plates.

On arriving at the next major station along the line, nobody had been permitted to leave the train until after the local peace officers and officials of the railroad had conducted an inquiry into the incident and carried out a search of all the travelers' persons and belongings. Because of her forethought, nothing of any incriminating nature had been found on any of them and the "widow's weeds" she had on had ensured an undeserved sympathy. She had received so little attention that she could have had the loot, the now badly damaged leotard, and her weapons, as well as the means for making herself look as she had the last time she had contacted the fence—which she was compelled to have along so as to keep to the plan she had formulated—in her small amount of baggage without them being detected.

Being cautious by nature, at least where her own safety was concerned, Libby had been disinclined to take any more chances than were unavoidable, such as keeping the items needed for her disguise with her. Therefore, she had insisted all the garb used by herself and her associates while the robbery was taking place be thrown from the train after they had donned the more innocuous attire in which they were traveling. There could have been one snag to her arrangements in spite of the precaution, but this had not arisen.

Apart from his bulk drawing some attention his way regardless of his following the instructions he was given to dress in a similar fashion to the noncircus men who would be his closest traveling companions, being unarmed, there was nothing about Stanislaus Padoubny to make him noticeable or arouse suspicion. However, although their knives were found on them, the fact that the Martinelli brothers had refused to dispose of the knives aroused no interest or speculation when they were discovered, because many Italians often went armed in such a manner. The reddish-brunette had left her own knife, the Smith & Wesson, and the loot with Jinks, whose spirited and lifelike impersonation of a savage dog had prevented a close scrutiny of the container in which he was hidden.

Being at liberty to carry on after the abortive attempts to find the plates—or anything else to help learn who was responsible for the crime—were concluded, the reddish-brunette had insisted upon adhering to the schedule she had conceived. Once she and her associates had left the train, problems that she had suspected might happen had begun to arise. Not improved by Jinks's mocking behavior and reminders that the twins were an essential portion of his act, a duty forced upon them that neither had ever relished, there had been considerable animosity from them over her returning alone to Washington, D.C., with the loot for disposal to Lachlan as had been arranged. However, with the all-too-willing support of the midget clown and backed unthinkingly by the menacing muscle power of strong man Padoubny, she had succeeded in quelling their objections.

Because of the need for Libby to bring back something close to a more harmonious relationship between the men—although this had always been a fragile thing where Jinks and the twins were concerned—when she set off by the first available train, she had been in a less-than-amiable frame of mind. Traveling in the overwarm "widow's weeds" and the rest of her disguise—the delay while settling the disagreements between her associates having prevented her from changing into the attire and makeup worn on her first visit to Lachlan—had been made even more irksome than was the case on the outward journey. Therefore, being tired and still less than at her best on arrival in the capital city, she had failed to notice the headlines inscribed in large and generally red letters on the notices pinned to newsstands telling the supposed result of the robbery.

Because of the time required to make the necessary alterations to her appearance in the women's rest room at the depot and being engrossed by the thought of receiving the balance of the payment she was promised for delivering the plates, the reddish-brunette had reached the office of the fence without having discovered things were not going the way she had expected. Although she would have willingly gone through the accepted ritual before being admitted, she had seen Beagle going to answer the "call of nature" as she reached the head of the stairs, and had decided not to delay her entrance until he returned.

Being unaware of the true state of affairs, Libbey was

surprised by the less-than-amiable reception she was being accorded.

"You mean you didn't know?" Lachlan asked, his tone disbelieving as he raised his right hand from its proximity with the Colt Storekeeper Peacemaker revolver he kept in the drawer as a second line of defense for the Remington up his sleeve.

"What do I have to know?" Libby demanded, without showing an equal sign of relaxing and keeping the Smith & Wesson's barrel directed at the center of the fence's scrawny chest. "If it's about those two guards being shot, you must have realized from the beginning that it would have to be done."

"That hasn't anything to do with it, although it happening hasn't helped make matters any better," Lachlan answered, and waved a hand to the two newspapers lying unopened on his desk. "Take a look at what's said in these, if you haven't already seen them."

"They're only bluffing about the plates," the reddish-brunette stated, having contrived to read the accounts that were given in each paper without relaxing her watch on the fence to any great extent. Using her left hand, she extracted the items in question from her bag and laid them before him. "Take a look at these. Why the hell would they be carrying two complete sets if both are fakes?"

"Because it was wanted for the deception to look even more convincing."

"How do you know that?"

"The man who told me said that it was so, and he is in a position to know."

"Can you trust him not to be trying to throw you wrong?"

"He's never been wrong with anything he brought to me in the past," Lachlan asserted with complete conviction.

"And I've got too much on him for him to be deliberately trying to pull anything on me."

"It still doesn't seem right that they'd take so much trouble—!" Libby growled, glaring from the fence to the plates and back.

"Why not?" Lachlan inquired. "Like he said when he told me what he knows, with what's at stake, the government would want *every* possible precaution taken to make sure the real plates get to San Francisco safely. Do you have any idea what it would mean if they didn't?"

"Sure," Libby declared. "Somebody would be able to print up a heap of money that can't be told from the real thing."

"It goes far beyond that," Lachlan corrected. "The government will be in a hell of a bad state. The only way they could stop a disaster would be to call in all the paper money that's around already and replace it with some that's completely different. The moment that was started, there'd be a panic and everybody would want to start changing their paper cash for gold and silver currency. It could rip the whole economy of the country apart."

"And you want that," the reddish-brunette asked in a disbelieving tone, failing to see how there could be any profit in the situation for the fence.

"The people I'm working for d—!" Lachlan began, and stopped abruptly as he realized he was making an indiscreet response.

"Who would they be?"

"I can hardly—!"

"The hell you can't!" Libby snorted, then grinned. "Anyway, you don't need to. It's big businessmen, isn't it?"

"No," Lachlan denied, and, wanting to flaunt his superior knowledge before the woman who had so ably got the better of him on their last meeting and was far less respectful than any other criminal with whom he had come

into contact, went on. "It's a bunch of wealthy 'liberals'—
or they claim to be that way in the hope of winning votes
from the workingmen that they would need to get elected
into political office—who know their only hope of taking
control of the country is by discrediting both the elephants
and mules, which would happen when word leaked out, as
they would see it did, about the paper currency being un-
safe because of the counterfeit they'd put on the market."

"They must have plenty of cash to throw around," the
reddish-brunette said pensively. "Can't they use these
plates?"

"Certainly not," the fence answered, his voice redolent
of bitterness, as he had already considered the possibility
and had it discounted by what he was told by the men who
hired him and his informant. "Both sets look all right at
first glance, but they've flaws that would let everything that
was printed from them be easily detectable. Anyway, this
is what they've told me to do."

Gathering up the plates as he was speaking, Lachlan
carried them to the still-lit stove and, expecting to hear a
protest from the woman, threw them inside.

Instead of raising the anticipated protest, Libby tucked
the Smith & Wesson into the waistband of her skirt and
crossed to shovel some coal from the scuttle into the
mouth of the stove.

"I know those damned things aren't like the jewelry you
tried to pull the old burning game on with me," the reddish-brunette said, dropping the small shovel and drawing
the revolver swiftly. "So we'll just let them stay where they
are until they're ruined, in case you're just trying to get out
of paying me for getting them. Which you're going to do."

"Why should I?" Lachlan yelped, without either he or
the woman realizing they had inadvertently played into the
hands of General Philo Handiman, who had hoped the

destruction of the genuine plates would happen in the mistaken belief that they were of no use.

"Because I've done my part of the deal," Libby declared. "And it's no fault of mine that you can't use what I brought you. So you're going to pay up. It's me or the law!"

"You daren—!" the fence croaked.

"Try me," the reddish-brunette challenged, oozing the confidence of one who knew she held an unbeatable hand. "I've written down *everything* about how the deal was arranged and—!"

"How did sh—?" Beagle began, entering and bringing the declaration to a halt as quickly as his own question was ended by the Smith & Wesson being turned his way.

"Don't you try anything!" Libby warned, directing the words at Lachlan and causing him to refrain from taking the action he was contemplating. "The letter's with a friend I can trust all the way, and it'll be sent to the law if anything should happen to me."

"Get out of the office altogether, damn you!" the fence snarled, having no doubt he was being told the truth and considering it inadvisable to let his employee learn too much about his present affairs. After checking that the order was obeyed, he turned his attention back to the woman. "They haven't paid me, so—!"

"The hell they haven't!" the reddish-brunette asserted. "You wouldn't go outside to buy a paper for anybody else unless you'd had the money for it on the barrelhead, so I want what's coming to me."

"There's a way you can get it—and more."

"How?"

"The real plates are going to be sent to San Francisco."

"So?"

"So, according to my informant—who I told you is in a good position to be able to have learned about it—the plan is that another fake set are going under a heavy escort,"

Lachlan explained, impressed by the completely ruthless
nature of the woman and her obvious planning ability. He
had decided that she might be able to help him out of the
serious state of affairs in which he had become involved;
the men who had hired him to bring off the theft of the
printing plates had been menacing on learning that the
otherwise successful result of the robbery had—or so it
was made to appear, although he and they were unaware
of this fact—proved to be of no use. "But, to avoid allowing
any further unfavorable sentiments being aroused by the
'liberal' newspapers over more lives being lost if there is
another attempt made to steal them, the genuine article is
going to be taken there by a roundabout route."

"Who'll be doing the taking?" Libby asked, noticing the
speculative way in which she was being watched.

"I can't—!" the fence commenced, not wishing to let
himself appear too eager to comply. Then he gave a shrug
and went on, "Why shouldn't I? It's going to be a woman
who Pinkerton's have had pretending to be a very rich girl
from Texas called Betty Hardin while she was watching
somebody at the Grand Republic Hotel."

"A *woman*?" the reddish-brunette queried in a disbelieving voice that did not arise from hearing of Belle Boyd's
supposedly being a member of the Pinkerton National Detective Agency, as this was a long-established myth arranged by General Handiman—with the willingly supplied
cooperation of that organization's current leader—as a
means of avoiding her official status from being discovered.

"Not just *any* woman," Lachlan corrected. "She's the
one they still call the Rebel Spy."

"Is she, now?" Libby purred. "I hear she's pretty good."

"She's better than just pretty good by all accounts," the
fence claimed. "So good, in fact, that it's been decided to
let her make the delivery without any escort that might
draw unwanted attention her way."

"Has it, now?"

"It has."

"Now, that is interesting," the reddish-brunette almost purred. "Have you any idea how she's going to do it?"

"I told you my informant was good," Lachlan pointed out, his whole bearing redolent of the satisfaction he was feeling over having aroused such interest from his visitor that she had allowed the revolver to dangle by her side. However, with what he was hoping to achieve, he made no attempt to take advantage of this. "She's going out to a place called Ellsworth by train. It's the most eastern of those Kansas trail-end towns—!"

"I *know*!" Libby interrupted with impatience. "But why's she stopping there instead of keeping headed straight to 'Frisco?"

"That's the smart part," the fence replied. "She'll be going by stagecoach down to Texas and is being collected by a steam frigate at Galveston to take her by sea to San Francisco."

"That's a hell of a long way 'round," the reddish-brunette pointed out.

"As I said, that's the smart part," Lachlan answered. "The government are so determined to have the delivery brought off without any more trouble or killings that they don't mind the delay. So she'll be going to Texas in a way that nobody will think there's anything out of the ordinary."

"What's that?" Libby asked.

"She'll still be pretending to be this Betty Hardin who's now on her way to her home on a ranch in Rio Hondo County," the fence explained. "That way, nobody will suspect the truth and there won't be any need for her to have an escort."

CHAPTER TEN

THEY'RE *ALL* DEAD!

"So *you've* come back, have you?"

Even before Libby Craddock heard the words being directed her way in a savagely angry feminine voice she recognized, she had already sensed all was not well at the Circus Maximus.

Having accepted the offer made by Lachlan Lachlan of the McLachlans to steal what they believed would be the genuine set of currency printing plates that would be transported by Belle Boyd to San Francisco by taking a roundabout route, the only thing the reddish-brunette had required settling was how much carrying out the assignment would pay and what she was to receive in an advance. The latter had been the cause of some acrimonious debate before her claim that she needed money to cover the heavy expenses carrying out the robbery would entail was yielded to with very bad grace by the fence.

In fact, Lachlan had only surrendered to Libby's demand when she had pointed out—backed with a threatening gesture from her Smith & Wesson revolver, which she had not put away—she knew far too much about what was going on to be cut out of it. Therefore, she had said, because of what she knew, it was a case of her participating or she would inform the authorities of the scheme in such a way that she would avoid arrest for her part in the robbery and murder of the guards on the train. The fence had no doubt that she meant to keep her word and keeping in mind how she had told him there was a letter that would incriminate him waiting to be sent if he should succeed in having her killed. What was more, despite the dislike that had returned, he had felt sure she was intelligent and ruthless enough to produce the desired result.

Receiving the sum of money she required, the reddish-brunette had taken her leave of the fence. Being cautious and having no trust in him, she had kept a careful watch to her rear as she was taking a roundabout route toward the railroad depot. Before she had gone far, she had caught sight of Beagle following her. In one respect, the dishonest jockey could have counted himself lucky. Lying in wait for him in an alley, she had done no more than rendered him unconscious with the butt of her revolver instead—as was her first inclination—settling the matter permanently by using her knife. Satisfied that the way was clear for her to rejoin her companions without Lachlan being able to find her, she had boarded the appropriate train to let her catch up with the circus.

Confident it was safe for her to do so, shortly before arriving at the town where the next shows were to take place, Libby had taken her one suitcase into the rest room at the end of the car she was using. Having removed the makeup for the disguise and taken out the kind of clothing she wore for everyday use, she had done a quick change into it and put away the other garments. Then, waiting until she was given an opportunity to do so without being seen by the few passengers in the car, she went to her seat and, as an examination of the tickets by the conductor had taken place earlier, remained there unchallenged until the train came to a halt.

Much to her surprise, as she had told them at what time they could expect her to return, none of her four male accomplices were anywhere to be seen when she descended to the platform. While she had expected either Jinks or Stanlilaus Padoubny to be there so as to lend her a hand with her small amount of baggage, knowing why she had gone to Washington, D.C., she had thought the Martinelli brothers would be present if only to look out for their interests. Deciding against waiting in case there had been something to delay their coming, she went from the depot with the intention of making her own way to where she had been told the circus would be set up.

Because the small town did not offer the service of a cabriolet or any other similar type of vehicle plying for private hire, the reddish-brunette had to make her way to the circus on foot. Night had already fallen and, as she was drawing near, the first thing to strike her was how quiet everything was. There were the usual lights burning to illuminate the surrounding area, but the big top was in darkness and none of the usual music came to her ears. Nor, although the large and garishly colored balloon was inflated and anchored down ready for use, could she see anything to suggest even the sideshows were in operation.

Being aware that one had been planned for that evening, Libby wondered why Cosmo Caithness had elected to cancel the performance. She knew he was so pennypinching that only something of grave importance would have led him to miss the chance of taking in money. The reason could not be because she was absent, as, having studied the train schedules on arriving and been satisfied she could do so, she had obtained grudging permission from him for the others to fill in until she arrived in enough of her acts to pad out the bill and avoid complaints by the customers who attended about the brevity of what would otherwise take place. Caithness had not been eager to comply, but he knew how the success of his enterprise depended upon her various talents and dared not do anything to antagonize her in case this caused her to quit.

She swung around at the words, which she resented being directed her way in such a fashion no matter how justified the cause might be. What she saw gave her a slight sense of alarm. She was being approached in a distinctly hostile fashion by four of the women "flashers" who paraded around the ring, some wearing copies of her various types of attire, to give the impression that the show had far more actual performers than was the case. However, none of them were in any form of costume. Being aware that her assumption of superiority over them had always been the cause of resentment, she had been convinced that her status as a multistar performer—whereas none of them had the talent to perform even one—and the reputation she had acquired for being very dangerous to cross rendered her unlikely to be subjected to reprisals. Taking in the demeanor of the quartet, she concluded that this must have changed for some reason.

"Just who do you think you're talking to?" the reddish-brunette demanded, dropping the suitcase and slipping her right hand into the bulky bag to grasp the butt of the Smith & Wesson.

"You, of course," the largest of the four answered, being as Libby knew the one who had addressed her. "Who else?"

Equaling the reddish-brunette in height, good looking in a coarse way and with untidily piled-up hair that needed treatment to retain its blond hue, the woman was heavier. Furthermore, as she had to lend a hand with the work of setting up the big top in addition to other tasks calling for the employment of muscle power, there was little or no flabby fat on her Junoesque frame. In fact, she was the only one of the female employees of the circus whom Libby had always regarded as needing to avoid being pro-

voked into hostile action. Going by appearance, for some
reason she could not guess at, she might be given no
choice in the matter.

What was more alarming, the reddish-brunette sensed
from the way the other three "flashers" were eyeing her
with an equal animosity that if a fight started she might
not be in contention against only a single antagonist. To
add to her growing sense of consternation, she was aware
of just how dangerous coming under attack by the whole
group, or even the blonde under the circumstances, might
be. Even if she should prevail in single conflict and was
not subjected to a mass attack when this was seen to be
taking place, she stood a good chance of being left in no
condition to set off on the assignment from Lachlan as
soon as she must to have a chance of achieving a successful conclusion.

Yet a further source of trepidation for Libby came as
she realized that none of the men with whom she had
committed two robberies, ending in a double murder on
each occasion—the last time having been premeditated—
were anywhere to be seen. In fact, she was as puzzled by
their continued absence as she had been at the depot.
Knowing how they were all eager to find out how much
they had profited from the second robbery, she felt they
ought at least to have kept an eye open for her arrival at
the circus grounds and come to greet her. If they had, she
would now have nothing to fear from the "flashers."

The realization raised another deeply disturbing point
for the reddish-brunette.

Why were the women adopting such an attitude when
they must know they would be prevented from making an
attack, or stopped very quickly and painfully by the midget
clown and the strong man.

"What the hell do you four think you're doing?"

Libby could not remember when the sound of Cosmo Caithness's voice had been so pleasant to her ears.

Glancing away from the menacing quartet, the reddish-brunette saw with relief that the large and flashily dressed proprietor of the circus was coming toward her at a greater speed than usual. As was generally the case around the circus, he was carrying the long-handled buggy whip he used as a symbol of his authority and a means of enforcing his will upon recalcitrant members of his show—including the "flashers" on occasion—when they objected to doing what he wanted. Although normally he made an effort to retain an appearance of affluence, despite running on as close to a shoestring budget as it was possible for the moderately successful organization to keep, his attire had traces of a greater disarray than she had ever seen before. What was more, his left eye was discolored and swollen to an extent that it resembled a bluepoint oyster peeping from its shell.

"We thought—!" the blonde began.

"Then *don't*!" Caithness snarled, holding his tones down to a lower level than was usual. "Get to your quarters and leave the thinking to me. We've got enough trouble around here without you bunch adding to them."

"What's happening, Cosmo?" Libby asked after the quartet had shuffled away in a clearly far from liked retreat. As usual, she was trading upon her importance as a performer to use the circus owner's given name when everybody else addressed him as "Colonel Caithness"—the military rank being assumed as he had never served in any capacity with the army—or "sir" and went on, "It has to be something *bad* for those cheap tail-peddlers—!"

"It is something bad!" Caithness confirmed. "Only, I'm not going to tell you about it out here with *them* probably watching us."

"Who?" the reddish-brunette queried, knowing only

something of unusual magnitude could cause the generally bombastic man to behave in such a fashion.

"I'll tell you in my caravan," Caithness promised, the living quarters for such of the personnel and their families who were resident on the lot having been brought by train with the show's animals and equipment.

"What's this all about, Cosmo?" Libby asked, setting down the suitcase she had retrieved so as to have both hands free and using the right to once more grip the butt of the Smith & Wesson revolver. "And where are Jinks and Laus?"

"They're dead," the circus owner replied quietly, looking at where the reddish-brunette had put her hand and drawing the conclusion that he had best not try the tactics he had intended to use. "In fact, they're *all* dead."

"Who?" Libby could not resist inquiring, although she could guess the answer.

"Jinks, Padoubny, and the Martinellis," Caithness replied, as the reddish-brunette had anticipated would prove to be the case.

"How did it happen?"

"Lord only knows how it started. Probably that evil little bastard pushed the wops too far. Anyway, the first I knew of it was when I heard a hell of a commotion behind the big top. By the time I got there, Jinks was down, gutted like a stuck pig. Padoubny was just as badly carved, but he'd already busted Lou's neck and was choking Van. Before we could make him let loose by hitting him with tent stakes, Van was as dead as Kelsey's nuts and he went off a few seconds later. It couldn't have happened at a worse time."

"In what way?" Libby wanted to know, realizing from what she had heard that she now had nobody with whom to share the proceeds of the two robberies and having meant to handle the recovery of the currency-printing plates without assistance from any of the quartet.

"I had the local chief of police and the mayor's top errand boy in here to sweeten them up so there wouldn't be any beef should the gilpins and rubes start saying they'd been rooked at one of the sideshows," the circus owner explained in deeply bitter tones. "It might not have been so bad even then, as I got the feeling there were some sticky palms around that would take greasing, but it didn't stay in local hands. Some fellers with proof they came from the Treasury Department arrived and told me that, as they'd found out all four of them had been on the train that got robbed, they were going to search their quarters."

"And did they?" the reddish-brunette asked, relieved that she had refrained from splitting the proceeds of the robbery at the Grand Republic Hotel—despite the demands by the Martinellis that it should be done—and had it concealed in the safest place she could conceive.

"Yes and damned thoroughly at that," Caithness confirmed. "But, so far as I know, they didn't find anything." Then he studied Libby in a thoughtful fashion and went on, "*You* came up on the train with them, didn't you?"

"I did," the reddish-brunette confirmed coldly, and eased back the hammer of the revolver despite its double-action mechanism removing the need to do so. "What's wrong, Cosmo? Do you think we robbed the train?"

"I *never* think," Caithness stated, having heard the clicking from inside the bag and knowing how it was caused. "They asked me where you was and I said you'd left word there was the chance of picking up an act for us further up track, so you'd gone to look it over for me like you'd done before."

"That was good of you," Libby said dryly. She knew the information had not been supplied because of the long tradition among circus people never to divulge any information about one another to people outside their own circle, but because the bulky man was expecting to receive payment for his silence. However, she also felt sure that none of the others—not even the blond "flasher"—would have been more forthcoming because of the same unwritten code of silence. "What happened then?"

"The chief of police told me for us to move on as soon as we could, and they all left," Caithness replied. "But I saw a couple of the Treasury men keeping what they thought was secret watch across the way."

"Why did you have the place lit up?" the reddish-brunette inquired, having no illusions about the proprietor's disinclination to spend money if doing so could be avoided. "You surely didn't aim to put on a show *tonight*?"

"I could hardly do that," Caithness growled bitterly. "Even if the local bumpkins would come when word spread about what had happened, they wouldn't have put up for what I could put on. I hoped at least a few of them would come in so the boys in the sides could get at them, but none have so far."

"When are *you* pulling out?" Libby queried, studying the man's face with a coldly knowing expression that did not escape his notice any more than the emphasis placed on the third word had.

"I'm going to have the tear-down tomorrow and take to the road when it's over."

"Where are *we* headed next?"

"To the first town where we can pull in customers."

"Aren't we traveling by rail anymore?"

"Not until I can get more padding for the show," Caithness replied. "We haven't a whole heap to offer with those four gone, have we?"

"Not enough for it to be worth our while heading for the trail end towns," the reddish-brunette admitted, although she felt sure that the proprietor had no more intention of staying with the circus than she had. "Well, there's nothing any of us can do tonight, so I'm going to turn in."

"You couldn't make me a small loan, could you, Lib?" Caithness inquired, trying to look amiable and reducing the name in a way he had never done before. "I've had some heavy expenses, as you can well imagine."

"How small?" Libby asked coldly.

"Could you go as high as two thousand five hundred?"

"Where would I get that kind of money?"

"You've been on top wages all the time you've been with me and got 'em even though there's some who haven't, and you don't throw your cash around any too much."

"I haven't got that much," the reddish-brunette lied, there being a far greater sum in her bag and more hidden away.

"How much can you make it?" the proprietor asked, with just a suggestion of menace in his voice. "I've a lot more overheads than you do *now*, you know."

"Two thousand's top dollar," Libby stated, realizing what was implied by the stress put on the "now."

"I'll take it," Caithness accepted, being too wise to push his multistar performer any further.

"I'll give it to you in the morning," the reddish-brunette promised, employing apparent sincerity although she had no intention of being around to do so.

"You know the old circus tradition, Lib," the proprietor said archly. "It's *always* cash on the barrelhead."

"So it is," Libby accepted with a shrug. Then, taking from the bag what she estimated would be sufficient of the money to cover the payment without allowing the sizable remainder to come into view, she went on, "Here, count it out of this."

"This's real generous of you, Lib," Caithness declared

with blatantly false gratitude. "And you'll get it back as soon as things are running smoothly again."

"I'm sure I will," the reddish-brunette countered, exuding an equally false sincerity and feeling satisfaction over the means she had already decided to employ as an aid to making her escape.

Leaving the proprietor, Libby went straight to the small caravan that—driven by Padoubny when traveling by road and often shared with Jinks, who had possessed surprisingly satisfying sexual qualities despite his small size—she made her home. Although she remained alert for further trouble with the "flashers," there was none and, once inside, she began to make her preparations for departure. With all she considered necessary for her travels packed, she waited until certain everybody else would be asleep or away from the grounds on private business—probably to do with acquiring money from the locals by various means to cover the losses caused by the circus being closed.

Although much of the illumination had either been put out or died from lack of fuel, Libby knew her way around the never-changing layout well enough to be able to do with the light that remained and to have no need for the small bull's-eye lantern she was carrying with its front covered. First going to where the balloon was tethered, she checked as well as she could that it was ready for use and felt certain it was sufficiently prepared for her needs. Feeling the breeze that was blowing on her cheeks, she knew it would serve her purpose adequately and was even blowing in the direction best suited for her purposes.

Having placed her belongings in the basket, the reddish-brunette retained the lantern and the means to carry out her next intentions. These were pieces of meat she had been keeping in her caravan to be used in such an eventuality when setting off for the robbery at the Grand Republic Hotel and had meant to change in the morning as they were starting to make their presence felt to the nostrils. Next, she made her way to the small traveling cage that held the tiger used in the wild animal act. Without needing any more illumination than was available, she opened the lock with the pick she had known would do the trick. Already aroused by the pungent smell of the beef, the big cat was on its feet and left the cage to follow when she tossed them into the darkness.

"You *bastard*, Caithness!" Libby spat out furiously, having entered the cage and used the beam from the lantern cautiously so she could open the secret compartment in the seemingly solid floor to find it empty. Aware that neither the trainer nor his assistants knew of the hiding place, she knew there could only be one culprit responsible for taking the money received for the loot from the robbery at the hotel. "I hope you go up with the rest of your stinking show."

Leaving the cage in a fury, which she nevertheless refused to cause her to become careless, the reddish-brunette went swiftly from place to place around the grounds. At each one, she started a fire and watched with satisfaction on returning to the balloon as each began to grow with the speed allowed by the inflammable material and surrounding. There was only one more thing that needed to be done for her plan to succeed. Aroused by her yells of "Fire!" people came rushing from their quarters. Much to her relief, although she anticipated it would be the case, Caithness's first concern was for the big top. That, she decided, was all to the good and simplified what she meant to do next.

"Hey, fellers!" Libby called to a trio of burly roustabouts who were heading at a run for the nearest conflagration. Climbing into the basket of the balloon while speaking, she went on with a suitable urgency, "Turn her loose and

I'll take care of her until she lands and the Big Man can have her fetched back."

Being aware of just how big an attraction the balloon always was, the men showed no hesitation before complying. With a feeling of joy and not a little satisfaction over the way in which she had avenged herself upon Caithness for what had been blackmail regardless of how it was worded, Libby was carried into the air and sent westward at a reasonable pace that would put miles behind her before she was compelled to land.

The reddish-brunette was satisfied that the way was clear for her to locate and kill Belle Boyd so she could get the genuine currency-printing plates.

CHAPTER ELEVEN

YOU'RE ALL ON YOUR LONESOME

"It's all right, ole Nigger hoss. I hear 'em real good 'n' have for more'n a spell already, you no-account half-deaf goat!"

While speaking, slouching on his low-horned and double-girthed saddle—which would have informed anybody with knowledge of the cattle business west of the Mississippi River that he was almost certainly a Texan, albeit probably one of mixed blood—although only about halfway through Oklahoma Territory, the Ysabel Kid gave the impression of being a natural part of the landscape.

Six feet in height, with a lean physique that nevertheless offered more than just a suggestion of possessing whipcord strength and practically tireless energy, what could be seen of the Kid's hair from beneath his low-crowned and wide-brimmed J. B. Stetson hat was so black it seemed to shine darkest blue in some lights. Unless one took notice of his red-hazel eyes, which gave a strong hint that the impression was almost certainly erroneous, there was an almost babyish innocent cast to his handsome, Indian-dark features. With the exception of the walnut handle of his clearly aged Colt Model of 1848 First Model Dragoon revolver, which was turned forward for a low cavalry twist-hand draw at the right side of his gunbelt, and the ivory hilt of the massive bowie knife in its sheath on the left, everything he wore from headdress to boots—with lower heels than was mandatory for a cowhand, as his duties as a long-standing member of the floating outfit for General Jackson Baines "Ole Devil" Hardin's OD Connected ranch often entailed working for considerable periods on foot—was black. In addition to the weapons visible on his person, there was a magnificent-looking Winchester Model of 1873 rifle riding with its butt pointed ahead in the boot on the left side of his saddle.

The white stallion upon which the Kid was riding would have aroused interest and not a little envy no matter how many of its kind were nearby. Despite being a good seventeen hands, there was no suggestion of it being slow or clumsy for all its size. Rather, it conveyed the impression of being as agile and maneuverable as a cutting horse, combined with the speed and stamina of a pronghorn antelope. In fact, despite the saddle and bridle, which were indications of its domestic status, it carried itself with the authority and sense of power frequently seen when it was a *manadero* leading a herd of free-living mustangs under observation. Its appearance gave a guide to the ability of its rider. Unless he was a rider of the first water, no man could stay on its back for very long, much less sit so seemingly at complete ease, without winding up lying on the ground and, in all probability, being stamped into a bloody ruin as soon as this happened.

Although the Kid conveyed an impression of being totally relaxed, it would have been obvious to anybody who knew him well that he was as alert as his upbringing since early childhood had taught him to be and not entirely at ease.[1] On the other hand, despite the gist of the comment he made, he gave no indication of being aware of the three riders who had been following him since he left the town of Stillwater shortly after sunup. Instead, he continued to lounge on the big stallion's back with the casual grace and ease of one long experienced in all matters equestrian, as if he was so deeply engrossed in thought that he was completely uninterested in everything going on around him.

Nothing could be further from the truth.

Making the journey back to Rio Hondo County to resume whatever duties might be awaiting him as one of the OD Connected's floating outfit, circumstances having been such that he was doing so alone, the Kid had welcomed the diversion that came his way while he was staying overnight in Pawnee. A friend of long standing, United States Deputy Marshal William M. Tilghman—one of the so-called Three Guardsmen who were already making a good start in their efforts to reduce the lawlessness that was rife throughout the Indian Nation—had greeted him warmly when he entered the bar of the hotel where he had elected to spend the night rather than in a solitary state with the sky for a ceiling and ground as a mattress, so had no escape from the misgivings that were plaguing him.

Without any doubt, the Kid had never been so deeply perturbed by his behavior in all his life. Nor was he trying to tell himself in exculpation that the event that caused him to have the feelings and was responsible for a hitherto enjoyable time spent in Mulrooney, Kansas, deteriorating to such an extent that his hurried—even furtive—departure was justifiable. He was even unable to derive any satisfaction from telling himself that there was a very good reason why at least one of the floating outfit had to arrive at Bent's Ford as soon as possible if an unpleasant situation was to be avoided. All the time he was aware that he had deserted two men, both of whom were closer to him than brothers and with whom he had shared many dangers, to face something in which he could not bring himself to participate.

After having delivered a warning that no smuggling

would be tolerated in the Indian Nations, a jocular reference to the way in which the Kid had made a living before the death of his father during the War Between the States,[2] Billy Tilghman had turned the conversation to more general matters. Much to the Kid's relief, the deputy, knowing that members of Ole Devil's floating outfit sometimes went on assignments alone, did not ask why he was doing so. Instead, adhering to the code of the land, where dealing with the personal matters of law-abiding citizens—as the Kid now justifiably could claim to be—were concerned, he merely restricted himself to inquiring whether Dusty Fog and Mark Counter were in the best of health. Doing all he could to suppress the qualms of conscience stirred even more by the mention of his two closest *amigos*—whom he had deserted to face what he regarded as being the most dire of circumstances—the black-dressed Texan had just said they were both fine and dandy when he last saw them.

Seeking to change the subject in what would appear to be a natural manner, as he had not seen either around, the Kid had asked after the other two Guardsmen. Knowing him to be completely trustworthy in spite of being acquainted with some of the better kind of outlaws, some of whom he had met while smuggling along the Rio Grande before and during the War, Tilghman had not hesitated before explaining that Deputy U.S. Marshal Heck Thomas was somewhere in the Panhandle country searching for renegades peddling whiskey to the Indians and Deputy U.S. Marshal Chris Madsen was up around Muskogee trying to get a line on Bad Bill Doolin's gang.

Saying he would naturally be calling in at Bent's Ford and explaining the particular need he had to do so on this occasion, the Kid had remarked about the way its owner liked to engage in a session of quartet singing and how he had heard Madsen possessed a fine tenor voice, so would like the opportunity to hear it put to use in such a combination. Tilghman had admitted that his fellow peace officer was as good at singing as at enforcing the law, also was always willing to participate when there was no urgent duty needing to be done. Then he said he was aware of the Kid also being a better-than-average tenor and hoped he might one day be fortunate enough to hear them join together and, as his own voice was closer to the braying of a thirsty burro, render some of his favorite ballads.

It had not been until the two chance-met friends had finished with what they considered the social amenities and were sharing a meal in the hotel's dining room that Tilghman had mentioned anything about his own law-enforcement duties to the Kid. He said, looking at the Indian-dark Texan in a pointed fashion, that there was one problem to which he would have liked to devote his personal attention if he did not have a more pressing assignment along the short border between the Indian Nation and Missouri that he could not delay commencing under the prevailing circumstances.

A series of robberies were being committed south of Stillwater, with trail hands, returning to Texas after having completed cattle drives to the railroad towns in Kansas, as the victims. It was claimed by the victims that three men were the perpetrators. However, as they appeared to select their prey carefully, the only descriptions were that all were tall, dressed as cowhands, and had bandannas masking their faces. Such was the skill shown so far in choosing whom to rob, none of those who had lost money and property to them could even say with certainty what kind of weapons they carried other than that each restricted himself to a single revolver of some unidentified kind.

While Tilghman did not ask outright, he had hinted that any assistance the Kid might be able to render would be most welcome. As an experienced lawman, he was aware that there were those in Texas who would claim that the reason no positive action was being taken by the U.S. deputy marshals—specially appointed for enforcing the law outside the cities and towns of the Indian Nation—was that all the victims had their origins in the Lone Star State. Although he had admitted such might be the case with some of them, the Three Guardsmen and the majority of their contemporaries would never be so neglectful of their duties on such grounds. In fact, several had also been born and raised between the Rio Grande and the border with Oklahoma. Then he had pointed out that so far the gang had restricted themselves to pistol-whipping the victim after delivering a warning for him not to try to put the law on their tail.

Having been assured that the Kid did not subscribe to such a negative point of view, which he had already been certain would prove to be the case, the deputy said he considered it was only a matter of time before the trio went too far and killed the man they were robbing. Knowing the suggestion was a distinct possibility, the Kid had promised to do what he could. He had added the proviso that he could not stay around Stillwater more than a couple of days at the outside, as he had an urgent reason for reaching Bent's Ford with the least possible delay. On hearing why this was so, the deputy had agreed that life would be a whole lot easier for him if he made the rendezvous at the appointed time.

Putting to use the knowledge acquired while serving in the capacity of deputy for Dusty Fog as a town marshal on two occasions, by the time he reached Stillwater, the Kid had decided how he might bring about the desired effect.[3] In the kind of coincidence no author of fiction dare employ in a plot, he had met an acquaintance upon whom he had felt certain he could depend to support him in his plan. Learning what was expected of him, the most inaccurately named Dude had immediately and willingly offered his assistance.[4] Agreeing that he would be unlikely to be taken for the kind of easy victim previously sought by the robbers, despite the fancy attire he always wore, which accounted for the only name by which he was known, he declared his confidence in being able to produce the result that would be required of him.

Although the Kid realized he would not be considered suitable for the same reasons as Dude under normal circumstances, he had made a significant change to his appearance that he hoped would serve his needs. Wanting to be sure he could not be mistaken for a more suitable candidate who might be passing through Stillwater, he retained his all-black garb. However, he made a change to his visible armament by removing the bowie knife and its sheath from his gunbelt to leave them with his most distinctive Winchester rifle—which bore the proud designation "One of a Thousand"—in the room he had taken at the town's best hotel.[5]

Making a round of the saloons and other places where the trio of robbers might locate their victims, the Kid had flourished what appeared to be a large wad of money. In reality, this was no more than carefully shaped pieces of newspaper with a couple of ten-dollar bills at the top and bottom. Following him on each occasion after he had left, without letting any indication of their association be apparent, Dude had announced loudly that he was just a damned half-breed who was not even a cowhand and not only worked as a horse wrangler—considered a person of much lower standing by the men handling the cattle on a trail drive despite having a most important function to perform—but would not even spend his earnings when paid off to buy something better than the ancient Colt Dragoon he carried. The impression left by Dude was that he considered "Billy-Sam" to be no more than a cheap pennypincher and a considerable coward when put to a test.

On leaving Stillwater that morning, putting to use the training in such matters he had received during his childhood spent exclusively with his maternal grandfather, Chief Long Walker—his father having spent much time away on the family business of catching mustangs combined with smuggling—in the village of the Pehnane Comanche, the Kid soon began to believe that his ploy was going to pay off. He had also been grateful that the need to keep far more alert than he gave the impression of being was causing him to put aside his feeling of misgiving over the way he had deserted Dusty and Mark Counter back at Mulrooney.

Before the Kid was a mile on his way toward Bent's Ford, where he would find the excuse he intended to use for the shoddy way he had treated his two *amigos*, he had detected distant signs of being followed by somebody. Taking into account the way in which whoever they might be were taking care to try to remain out of his range of vision so he could not make out how many riders there were, other than there being more than one, he had continued on his way without letting any indication of knowing they were there be detectable.

By the time his big white stallion gave the signal, to which he responded in a mocking fashion, the Kid had established that the followers were three in number. What was more—although he was not aware of the fact due to the small amount of information Tilghman had received about the way in which the robberies were carried out—he was very close to the area in which they had always made their move. All he knew was that they had come to such a close distance without allowing him a clear view of them that he felt the time was at hand when he must take some form of action against them. He was also pleased that certain arrangements he had made prior to leaving

Stillwater were still known only to him. Scanning the terrain, he found what he was looking for about a mile ahead.

APART from being tallish and skinny in build, Tony Lennon, Tom Loflin, and John Birt had two other traits in common. They had come from similar middle class–middle management backgrounds. Having proved incapable of holding down any employment that their respective families had considered suitable and refused to accept other jobs they regarded as being below their social scale, each was sent west to live on what in England was called a remittance, with the proviso generally imposed there that they not return home.[6] Every one of them had a desire to acquire sufficient money to live in a manner they felt they deserved without needing to do any kind of work. That was why they had elected to start robbing such Texas cowhands who were passing through Stillwater and met their requirements where the possibility of dangerous resistance was concerned.

While the trio were looking out for likely prospects the previous night, so well had the Ysabel Kid played his role and Dude helped to create the desired impression, they had decided he was the one best suited to their purpose. They had already considered and discarded Dude because, in spite of how he dressed suggesting to the contrary, they had believed he would prove too dangerous to be chosen as a victim. However, none of them had doubted that a half-breed employed as nothing more than a horse wrangler and armed with just an ancient cap-and-ball revolver would offer all the qualities they were seeking.

Satisfied that they had nothing to fear from their intended victim, the trio had followed him to the small hotel and heard him tell the clearly uninterested clerk on the reception desk that he would be checking out around seven the following morning so he could fetch his horse from

Whitley's livery barn and get on his way back to Texas. Although they hated to rise so early, they had considered that the size of the bankroll they had seen him flourishing made it worth their while to do so. If they had been more perceptive, they might have changed their opinion about the harmless nature of the black-dressed "half-breed" from the quality of his huge white stallion and the fine-looking Winchester rifle in his saddle boot.

Lacking the perception to draw the required conclusions, the trio had stuck to the procedure that had proved successful on every previous occasion—except that Lennon had been compelled to knock out the last victim with the barrel of his Colt Cavalry Model Peacemaker revolver when the first resistance they had encountered occurred—by following at what they believed was a distance preventing them from being detected by their quarry. They had gradually closed the distance and knew they would soon be arriving at the place where they had found surprise could be most easily attained. Showing a perception and ability that would have surprised their parents, confident that their presence was still unsuspected as they had neither seen nor heard anything to suggest otherwise, they attained the position from which they put in their appearance. Pulling up their bandannas so that they served as masks, it being their practice to always wear the clothing of town dwellers when not on their forays to lessen arousing the suspicions of the local constable—a man who they grudgingly conceded was possessed of some perception—each drew his revolver, ready for commencing the robbery.

HAVING previously been employed against young cowhands who were returning from a first trail drive and had had little experience of life before setting out, the system employed by the trio had never failed to achieve the effect they desired.

However, on this occasion they were in contention against the grandson of Chief Long Walker and a member of the Pehnane Comanche dog soldier war lodge in his own right. Furthermore, not only did he remember all he had been taught so he could attain that highly esteemed estate, his way of life since those days had never been so pacific that he *could* forget anything he had learned. Rather, he had refined the techniques to a high degree of competence.

The moment the Kid saw the clearing in the area of high and dense undergrowth through which he had been passing while the trio were closing the gap separating them, he knew this would be the place where their attempt at robbing him was made. Gambling upon his judgment and concluding that nothing would be lost should it be wrong, he made ready to handle the situation.

Being disinclined to count upon the Dragoon, be-cause—lacking the skill with a short gun possessed by both his *amigos*—he regarded it as a defensive weapon with only a slightly greater range than the bowie knife that was in the bedroll attached to the cantle of his saddle, the Kid bent down to grasp the wrist of the butt and slid out the Winchester. As it came clear of the saddle boot, he twisted himself clear of the stallion's back. At the signal he gave, the big white increased its gait and, by the time he was standing facing in the direction from which they had come, it was going out of sight along the path through the bushes at the other side.

Entering the open space with their weapons out ready, the three would-be robbers received a severe shock. In-stead of riding along completely unaware of their coming, their supposed victim was standing some twenty yards away, facing toward them with a superb-looking rifle— which would have been the best piece of loot to fall into their hands so far, provided they could take it—dangling

downward in an almost negligent-seeming fashion at arm's
length before him. Reining their horses to a halt, they were
too taken aback by the unanticipated turn of events to give
a thought to where the one the Texan was riding might be.

"Throw it down, beefhead!" Lennon commanded, using
the derogatory name he had heard used to describe Texans.
Although the other two would not have agreed, he regarded
himself as their leader, since he—acting more out of panic
than because he had thought of what to do on the spur of
the moment—had dealt with the attempt at resistance
shown by their last victim. As usual, he tried to make his
New England accent sound as if it was the voice of a man
born west of the Mississippi River. "There's *three* of us and
you're on your lonesome."

"Do tell," the Kid drawled, and snapped the butt of the
Winchester to his right shoulder and turning it into align-
ment with the speed many an exponent of the fast-growing
sport of shooting swift-moving birds on the wing would
have envied.

In the light of what happened next, the trio might have
counted themselves fortunate. In the days before he became a member of Ole Devil's floating outfit, the black-
dressed Texan—responding with the speed and frequently
literally deadly precision for which his Pehnane forebears
were famous—would not have hesitated to shoot to kill.
Now, because he suspected that his *amigos* did not look
with favor sometimes when he took such extreme measures, deciding that to do so might serve to lessen the
twinges of conscience still being experienced over the
shoddy way he had treated them, he aimed accordingly.

Selected in the order that the Kid decided they posed
the threat to him, he began to demonstrate the kind of
deadly skill and accuracy for which he had become famous
even prior to winning the "One of a Thousand" Winchester
as the first prize in a well-attended shooting match at the

Cochise County Fair in Tombstone, Arizona. Before any of them could try to even aim his way, Lennon received a bullet in the right shoulder. In very rapid succession, as the rifle's lever was put through the reloading cycle in a blur of motion, Loflin and Birt received similar wounds. Thrown from the backs of their horses, which responded in an instinctive restless fashion on being startled by the shots, the trio in turn landed and fell to roll on the ground screaming for mercy.

"You called it wrong," the Kid drawled, walking forward ready to deal with any attempt to make a hostile move against him even though he doubted one would be made. He could hear the drumming of hooves approaching in the distance and knew the arrangements he had made the previous day were being followed. "I'm still on my lonesome, 'cause you'll soon be headed back to Stillwater with the posse my *amigo* Dude 'n' the town marshal are fetching along."

---

1. *Details of the Ysabel Kid's birth, upbringing, and later adventures can be found in* APPENDIX TWO.

2. *How the Ysabel Kid avenged the murder of his father is told in* THE YSABEL KID.

3. *The periods when the Ysabel Kid and other members of General Hardin's floating outfit were required to serve as peace officers are recorded in* QUIET TOWN; THE MAKING OF A LAWMAN; THE TROUBLE BUSTERS; THE CODE OF DUSTY FOG *and* CARDS AND COLTS.

4. *Where the Ysabel Kid first met Dude is told in* TRAIL BOSS.

4a. *Dude makes "guest" appearances in* WEDGE GOES TO ARIZONA, ARIZONA RANGE WAR, *and* ARIZONA GUN LAW.

5. *How the Ysabel Kid acquired the "One of a Thousand" Winchester Model of 1873 rifle is told in* GUN WIZARD.

6. *Information about an Englishman who appeared to have been sent to the United States in such a fashion is given in* THE RE-MITTANCE KID *and* THE WHIP AND THE WAR LANCE.

CHAPTER TWELVE

I CAN TELL YOU HOW YOU CAN MAKE A HEAP MORE MONEY

"If we play it the way I say," Jesse Wilbran asserted, paying no attention to what he believed to be nothing more than a drunken saloon girl sleeping with her head resting on her forearms at the next table, "we'll take that ole stagecoach without no trouble at all."

Having listened to the conversation so far, although in one respect she would have preferred more competent-looking assistants, Libby Craddock decided she would have to make do with the group upon whom she was eavesdropping.

On the other hand, the reddish-brunette—currently having a blond wig and appropriate attire—realized that the men to whom she was listening were sufficiently stupid to do what she would require of them without question, provided she handled them properly.

After all, Libby told herself, she wanted dupes with just enough intelligence to do what she needed rather than those capable of thinking for themselves.

Throughout the assignment she had taken on, the reddish-brunette considered she had met with considerable good fortune so far. With the balloon in the air, she was pushed just off a westerly direction by a steady breeze at around five to six miles per hour and carried away from the railroad track without going too far south. Back at the Circus Maximus, everybody was far too busy for some considerable time trying to cope with the fires she had started. Neither the show folk nor the fire brigade that came rushing from the town had their task made easier by needing to deal with the tiger she had turned loose so she could check on the secret cache in the bottom of its cage. While old, with practically no teeth left and its claws removed, it was still a dangerous proposition until armed police officers had come to shoot it.

When the conflagration was finally brought under control, with the big top completely gutted and much more damage inflicted, deducing from the tiger having been liberated that Libby had discovered that he had stolen the money she had stashed away, Cosmo Caithness had demanded that she be found and brought to him so he could be avenged in a most painful way upon her. Realizing belatedly what they had done, the three roustabouts made no mention of the way they had helped her get the balloon into the air. Instead, they claimed that they had seen it rising and thought their boss set it adrift to save it from the flames.

On daylight coming, the reddish-brunette had found herself over fairly open country with no sign of human habitations in the immediate vicinity. Waiting until she located a small town in the distance, she used her knowledge to bring the balloon to earth behind a wooded area far enough away to avoid any chance of an early riser seeing its descent. Safely down, she had removed all her property and set light to the means by which she had escaped. When satisfied that there was nothing left by which it might be recognized for what it had been, she concealed all she had brought with her except the means to make a change to her appearance.

Putting what she regarded as being sufficient money for immediate needs along with her weapons in the bulky handbag, the reddish-brunette had made her way to the town. Her arrival on foot came at an hour when few people were about, and she attracted no attention. Going to the livery barn, she had found only one elderly man in attendance and asked to rent a buggy in which she could go supposedly to fetch back her husband who was lying injured in an accident about a mile away. Her story was believed, and the man insisted upon accompanying her as a driver and to render any other help she might require. His kindness was repaid shortly before reaching the woodland by having the knife that had taken the life of the maid at the Grand Republic Hotel thrust into his back and killing him instantaneously. With his body hidden and her property aboard, she had had the means to return to the railroad and take a westbound train.

Nothing of interest had taken place during the journey to Ellsworth, Kansas. However, on arrival, Libby had had what she considered to be her best piece of luck so far. Wondering how she could locate Belle Boyd, or find out if the Rebel Spy had reached the trail end, she had found herself at a facility offered for travelers by the railroad. A large room behind the depot was used to allow passengers going to areas where the tracks did not reach to have their baggage stored or taken to whatever means of transport they would be using to get there.

Looking around on the pretense of searching for her own property, the reddish-brunette could hardly believe her good fortune when she saw half a dozen fair-sized, expensive-looking pigskin suitcases all of which bore labels inscribed, "Elizabeth Hardin, OD Connected Ranch, Rio Hondo County, Texas, Via Bent's Ford, Oklahoma." They were in a section given over to the Wells Fargo & Company and the information that they would be required to be delivered to their depot four days later in time to be loaded aboard a southbound stagecoach.

Remembering how one of the other sets of plates had been hidden, Libby had wondered whether the same means might be used and if she could effect an entry to the building that night and carry out an examination. However, after questioning one of the attendants on the pretense of being worried about the safety of some expensive property she was expecting and might be delayed in collecting, she had been assured there were men on duty twenty-four hours a day and the last intruders had been shot before they could achieve anything. Accepting that she would not be able to accomplish anything in that direction, she had concluded she might be better advised not to try to carry out her assignment in Ellsworth. Instead, she had given thought to how she might achieve her purpose in another way—to allow the other woman to be well on the journey to Texas without anything happening, which might arouse a sense of false security and lead to a lessening of vigilance.

However, the reddish-brunette considered that one way of achieving her purpose could be ruled out. Lachlan Lachlan of the McLachlans had warned the reddish-brunette that Belle Boyd was a very sure and competent woman who would be unlikely to take chances while engaged upon such a mission. Therefore, she might be suspicious of a chance-met woman who tried to strike up an acquaintance. With that in mind, Libby had sought for the means to make the most of the start she would have and arrive at an area where a suitably relaxed state of mind had been reached.

Going to the Wells Fargo office without using a disguise, knowing she would get better results by applying her charms to the men employed there, the reddish-brunette had learned enough about the way her victim would be traveling to feel satisfied that she could reach the vicinity of Bent's Ford in time to locate whatever assistance she might require. From what she had been told about the arrangement to safeguard the passengers, she concluded she would not be able to achieve her purpose unaided. Instead, she would have to make the attempt somewhere along the way. However, she did not believe that traveling on the same stagecoach would supply the answer when dealing with someone as smart as she heard claimed Belle Boyd could be expected to prove. Instead, she had to get ahead of it and select somewhere suitable for attaining her purpose. Nor did she consider that these purposes would be beyond her abilities to achieve.

Among other talents Libby had acquired in her life spent around circuses was an expertise as a horsewoman, and she had had considerable experience at sitting astride. Obtaining two good mounts with which to ride relay in the way she had heard described by men of the West whom she had met in the East, she had impressed the owner of the livery barn from which she purchased them with her knowledge of exactly what she required. As a result of this, she had acquired animals that would cover a good distance at a faster speed than a stagecoach would be moving while still retaining a reasonable trade in value when they became tired along the way. She also acquired male clothing, in which she could travel and attract less attention than would be the case if she went openly as one of her sex.

One snag that Libby had failed to take into account when agreeing to go after the currency-printing plates was how to get the assistance she would acquire. While the largest in the matter of loot acquired, the two robberies she had planned and put into effect were not the first crimes in which she had engaged. In fact, making use of the traveling she did with various circuses, she had augmented her earnings by this means ever since she was old enough to plan and carry out crimes. In addition to having been able to call upon the services of Jinks, Stanislaus Padoubny, and, later, the Martinelli twins, she had formed connections with criminals throughout the eastern side of the United States, which allowed her to locate and obtain any other help she had required. She had belatedly become aware that the same did not apply west of the Mississippi River. If she had not been compelled by circumstances to rush into the task she had accepted, she could have been able to obtain information to help her locate others of her kind. However, from all she had learned about the condition of lawlessness that prevailed through much of the Indian Nation, she had felt sure she could overcome the difficulty.

By riding relay, dressed in suitable male attire and with her skill at applying makeup to help her pass muster on the few occasions when she had to come into contact with other human beings, Libby carried all her belongings except the Smith & Wesson revolver and knife—which were on the Western-style gunbelt she had obtained with the clothing—in a tarpaulin-wrapped warbag on one of her saddles. Putting into use all the skill she possessed, she covered ground at a good speed and estimated that she was sufficiently far ahead of the stagecoach carrying her victim to have time to seek out the assistance she felt sure she was going to need.

One thing the reddish-brunette had soon discovered as a result of her dealings with the owners of livery barns when the time came to change horses was that they and their hostlers were exceptionally useful sources of information and, provided they were handled correctly, were willing to disburse it. Taking advantage of Oklahoma City's having a sufficiently large population for strangers to be less likely to arouse comment than in a smaller town, having decided the time had come to try to find out where outlaws might be contacted, she set about doing so.

Changing into her feminine attire and putting on an appearance of concern, Libby had told the owner of the livery barn that she was negotiating for her younger brother, who was going on an important business trip and that she wanted to ensure he did not go places where he might fall in with bad company. Hearing the "brother" was traveling toward Bent's Ford, the man had said Big Win's Place just outside the small town of Cherokee was one definitely to be avoided, as many unsavory characters were frequently to be found there. Learning the reason for its name and where it could be located, saying she would deliver a warning that it must be avoided, she had taken her departure. Making a purchase in a store that apparently did much business with the kind of person she felt she would obtain the result she wanted by pretending to be, she had continued the journey after resuming her masculine garb.

On arriving at Cherokee, having located her destination in a small grove of trees a short distance away, the reddish-brunette was so convincing in her male role by now that she had no difficulty in hiring the only horse and buggy available at the livery barn on the grounds that her relay needed a rest while she attended to some business in the vicinity. On leaving town, she had changed into the garments and cheap jewelry bought for her intention to appear as a saloon girl in search of employment. The place at which she arrived proved to be a large wooden building with half a dozen shacks and a corral around it. On being admitted to what proved to be a large and not expensively furnished barroom, she was not impressed by what she saw until noticing that there were some better grades of whiskey in bottles on the shelves behind the counter. The discovery made her realize that the place must attract a more lucrative kind of customer than seemed to be the case at first sight.

Living up to her name, Big Win proved to be a massive woman in her late fifties and showing signs of what had been a considerable beauty in her younger days. She had also proved to be very perceptive by stating that Libby was not what she appeared to be on the surface. When ordered to tell the truth that she was not what she pretended to be, giving an assurance that she had done nothing to cause the Three Guardsmen or other peace officers to come hunting for her and giving her name as "Katey Smith," the reddish-brunette claimed she had been told to come and wait for a boyfriend to join her. Much to her relief, she found that Big Win knew something of the crooked gambler called Last Card Johnny Bryan, whose acquaintance she had made while he was working in the East. Saying she could remain and help out around the bar, but not to expect to be paid, the woman had left her there to make a visit to Cherokee.

There had been no customers for some time. The only bartender who remained had taken to heart the reddish-brunette's warning that Last Card Johnny would be very angry should she complain about having been bothered in any way and left her to her own devices. Although she had hoped for a better prospect, none had shown when six young men arrived. If she had known more about conditions in the West, although each wore a gunbelt of the kind she wore for use in her masculine persona, she would have seen that their clothing was an admixture of town and country garments. Of various heights and builds, the men were in their early twenties.

Studying the new arrivals, Libby had concluded they were much like eastern criminals of the same kind she had known. Therefore, if she had not known there was little enough time to make arrangements for dealing with Belle

Boyd, she would not have been inclined to consider them as potential assistants. However, acting as if already drunk, she had discovered they did not require anything other than a beer apiece. Collecting a bottle of cheap whiskey from the bartender and giving him a five-dollar bill with the instruction to mind his own business, she went to sit at the table next to the group. Giving a pretense of falling into a drunken sleep, she found their conversation most interesting.

"We didn't do all that well on the last three stickups we pulled, Jesse," protested the shortest of the group. Tony Blair was a stocky and unprepossessing-featured youngster in unclean cowhand clothing who Libby guessed was cultivating a stubbly growth of mouse-brown whiskers in the hope of making him look older and tougher than was the case. "By the time we cut the take between us, there wasn't more'n we could've made working cattle."

"They was only mud wagons," Wilbran replied. Taller than any of his companions by a couple of inches and better built, he had reddish hair and a handsome face with dissipation in its lines. He was the best dressed, with the attire of a cow-country dandy limited only by his means and carrying a pair of white-handled Colt Civilian Model Peacemakers on a gunbelt that looked as if it was intended to allow a fast draw. "The Wells Fargo stage down to Bent's'll be carrying folks with a whole heap more cash on 'em than the nesters and such's we took from."

"And it'll have a feller riding shotgun with a twin-barreled ten-gauge," sullen-featured, unshaven, and burly Jack Cunningham pointed out. Second to Wilbran in height and heft, his garments suggested he could be classed as a nester rather than a ranch hand. "All them Wells Fargo stages do."

"We pull it the way I've fixed for us to and he won't get him a chance to use it," Wilbran claimed coldly, knowing the other was a rival for leadership of the gang he and his younger brother Sim had formed. "And anyways, them shotguns're told not to raise any fuss if doing it'll put the passengers in danger."

"We don't know's how there's going to be any passengers on it," Frank Dobson reminded, ever a pessimist.

"There'll be at least one," Libby stated, rising and crossing to the next table. Startled exclamations burst from all the young men, and they began to shove back their chairs. Glancing at the counter and seeing that the bartender was watching without giving any indication of leaving his place, she went on, "Settle down. We're all in the same game and I can tell you how you can make a whole lot more money than by just taking whatever cash the passengers have with them."

"How?" asked Simcock Wilbran, a slightly younger and not quite so well dressed version of his brother.

"There's a woman called Elizabeth Hardin coming down on it," the reddish-brunette explained as the men sank back on their seats. "She's from one of the richest families in Texas, so all you have to do is take her along with you to some place and hold her for ransom. They'll pay real high to get her back."

"Who the hell are you?" Cunningham snarled.

"That's no way to talk to a *lady*!" Jesse snapped, knowing the other to be a threat to his leadership. Then he swung his gaze to Libby and went on in a more polite tone. "But he does have him a point, ma'am."

"I'm Belle Starr," the reddish-brunette said in a quietly impressive tone, using a name—which had featured so prominently in highly spiced stories that were circulated back east—she felt certain would produce the effect she required.

"Belle—!" Sim began, looking respectful.

None of them had become curious about the accent of

the "blonde" giving no sign of such origins. Even Cunningham showed that he, too, was impressed by meeting somebody who claimed to be the famous lady outlaw who made Oklahoma her home.

"But you can call me Katey Smith," the reddish-brunette stated rather than suggested. "It's a game I've been thinking on, and I was looking for a smart bunch like you to help me pull it off. That's why I came to Big Win's." Her gaze went to Jesse and her tone changed until it sounded respectful as she went on. "How do *you* figure on taking the stage, Jesse?"

Puffing out his chest more than a little at the way in which the "famous lady outlaw" had clearly chosen him as the undisputed leader of the gang, saying they had worked before and his examination of the route had located a place where the required conditions were available, the would-be dandy explained the means to be employed. Without realizing that the way selected had been learned from a blood-and-thunder booklet called "Jesse James, Gentleman Bandit," Libby was most impressed by what she heard and decided the gang might serve her purpose after all. At the conclusion of the explanation, she told how the kidnapping was to be carried out and was informed that a hideout was available where the victim could be held until the ransom money was forthcoming.

Calling for a round of drinks, the reddish-brunette felt highly delighted by what she believed she had achieved. Once her instructions were carried out, she could search the baggage in which she felt sure Belle Boyd was carrying the printing plates. With them in her possession, she would leave her dupes to wait for the ransom that would never come. While the authorities and the Pinkerton National Detective Agency—to which organization she had been told the Rebel Spy belonged and so would be determined to bring to justice whoever was responsible for her

fate, likely to be death after rape once it was discovered
she was not Elizabeth Hardin and no money would be paid
for her return—were hunting for them return to Washington, D.C. Once there, Libby was confident she could locate the "liberal" backers of the scheme and cut Lachlan
out of the deal altogether. What was more, she thought—
with her four associates from the circus dead—she would
be able to keep the whole of the money she acquired for
herself.

CHAPTER THIRTEEN

YOU'RE COMING WITH US, MISS HARDIN

Facing forward in the left-side corner seat of the Wells Fargo stagecoach made by Abbot & Downing in New England that would be arriving at Bent's Ford shortly before sundown, Elizabeth "Betty" Hardin decided—while it might offer the swiftest way of traveling by transport available to the public from Ellsworth there was currently available—it was far from the most comfortable way in which she had ever made a journey.[1] The best she could say about it was that the good condition in which the company ensured the trail was kept allowed them to cover around twenty-five miles a day. There were other things that caused her to feel a better means of completing the trip home would be vastly preferable.

For one thing, although the situation was now alleviated, Betty had not been enamoured of the crowded conditions that had to be endured due to there being a full complement of fifteen passengers—five each facing forward and to the rear, with the remainder occupying a removal bench across the central aisle—aboard in the earlier stages. Never a snob, she had accepted having to sit "dovetailed" with her legs between those of the woman facing her in the center. Nor had she demanded or even expected preferential treatment either while traveling or staying overnight at the way stations along the route on account of her social standing in Texas.

A major source of annoyance for Betty had been the presence of a passenger who insisted upon trying to be the life and soul of the party regardless of the feelings of his fellow travelers. Big, burly, well dressed, with a florid face redolent of bonhomie, which was probably an asset in his business of salesman for a major general-goods store in the East, Harold Goodgold—he insisted upon referring to himself by the horrible pun "Good As"—who insisted without the least encouragement on her part as considering himself to be her protector against each and every discomfort. Such an attitude would have been found amusing by the crew of the OD Connected ranch if they had seen it. The general consensus of opinion among them would have been that their well-liked "boss lady" needed slightly less protection in any circumstances than a momma Texas flat-headed grizzly bear—accounted by them, as loyal sons of the Lone Star State, despite the lack of any scientific corroboration, as being the largest and most dangerous of the species *Ursus horribilis*—fresh out of hibernation and with young cubs along. Much to her disappointment, having claimed he was headed west from Bent's Ford to let folks that way see what they were missing, he was still accompanying her.

Being fair-minded, although not approving of the motive, Betty had had to admit to herself that she was at least partly to blame for the interest Goodgold had taken in her. Even without her position and standing in Texas, which he had clearly known, she was by far the most attractive member of her sex making the journey. However, apart from both having the same-color hair and being beautiful, there was no way in which Belle Boyd could have been accepted as her by anybody who had made her acquaintance, and, fortunately for the deception, if any such person had been in Washington, D.C., their paths had not crossed.

Only five feet two in height, being less willowy than the Rebel Spy, Betty had an appearance that only a confirmed misogamist or a sexual deviate would not have found most pleasing to the eye. Tanned without having become harshened by the sun of her native Texas, her smooth-skinned features were as near perfect as any woman could expect. However, there was a suggestion of strength of will—without arrogance—and the saving grace of good humor about them. Her long-lashed eyes were coal black and met a man's without distrust or promise. Rather, they were a further indication that she was a capable and self-controlled young woman who could be grimly determined when the need arose.

Having removed and hung her black J. B. Stetson Texas-style hat by its fancy *barbiquejo* chin strap on a hook provided for that purpose brought Betty's hair, which was kept cut fairly short for ease of care in her active life, into view. Her figure was rich and full, eye-catching without being in any way flaunting or provocative. Tailored for the purpose, neither her black bolero jacket nor frilly-bosomed white silk blouse drew attention to the swell of the bosom they concealed. Nor did her black divided skirt, intended to permit riding astride rather than sidesaddle, give more than a suggestion of the trim hips and shapely legs underneath. Her ensemble was completed by high-heeled, sharp-toed, and fancy-stitched boots of the kind worn by cowhands and had Kelly spurs attached to them.

Although neither showed similar attention to Betty, she had soon concluded that the only two of the passengers on the final leg of the journey were not much of an improvement on the salesman as far as traveling companions went. One was Russel Prouty, a portly, soberly clad, stuffy, and prosperous-looking businessman who had boarded at the last town along the route. Obviously fully aware of his own importance, he had remained aloof and showed he had no liking for Goodgold's attempts at finding everything that happened a source of humor. Nor was Gilbert Griffin any more sociable company. Poorly attired, he had the appearance of being the kind of nester who tried to wrest a living from soil ill-adapted for his kind of agriculture. Lean, gaunt, and mournful of demeanor, he bore himself like one who had all the cares of the world on his shoulders. Eating and drinking sparely along the way, he had reacted with a horrified refusal when offered a cigar and asked to partake of the whiskey from the salesman's hip flask. All in all, Betty had assumed he was clearly close to the blanket as far as money went. His only brief entry into conversation had been to comment on the poor state of farming in Kansas and how little he was able to scrape up for his place so he could try his luck in Oklahoma.

Even before being inflicted by Goodgold's bonhomie and learning she would no longer have Goodgold's company to contend with after Bent's Ford, Betty had decided that she would acquire something more to her liking in which she could continue the journey to the OD Connected ranch in Rio Hondo County, Texas. After having been notified by telegraph of her intentions and the hope that they could accompany her, she felt sure she could depend upon the ranch's trail crew at Mulrooney, Kansas, to make it their business to do so. In addition to their having to be going back to the spread anyway at the conclusion of their successful delivery and sale of a herd of cattle, she felt sure they were all too aware of the way in which she would react on their next meeting should they fail to do as she had requested.

Although Betty was a highly placed member of one of the richest families in Texas, her attitude did not arise out of being a pampered and spoiled brat demanding that everything be as she desired. Apart from her grandfather, General Jackson Baines "Ole Devil" Hardin, there was nobody in the world she respected and cared for more than the men she had contacted. However, while no older than they, she regarded each—even her cousin and *segundo* of the OD Connected when not engaged upon some activity as a member of the floating outfit, Dusty Fog—as unruly young brothers who needed to be kept under control to prevent them from getting into mischief.

It must be said in exculpation of Belle Boyd that she would never have chosen to select the name of a good friend, with whom she had on one occasion shared a very dangerous situation,[2] in the deception upon which she was engaged if she had known Betty would actually be taking a departure from Ellsworth at such a critical stage of its performance. The plan had never been for her to go to Texas and "around the Horn" to California.

Instead, after having established that her *alta ego* was in that city, Belle was to take a westbound train in a way that it was hoped would cause those who were after her some considerable expense to locate and follow her.[3] She had, in fact, gone ahead with the scheme as planned without even bothering to go near the Wells Fargo depot—the booking of the journey being carried out through the hotel at which she was staying and, for some reason, there having been no mention from the clerk who made the arrangements that a person with the same name and address had already departed—and discovering she could have inadvertently placed Betty in what might easily prove to be grave danger.

WANTING to avoid being subjected to any more supposed wit from Harold Goodgold, Betty Hardin was gazing out of the window of the stagecoach as if finding the passing terrain of interest. In fact, the brush- and tree-lined area through which the trail was moving along the line originally taken by enormous herds of buffalo—which invariably selected the easiest and best-watered passage in the course of their migrations—had already grown so repetitious that she would have found it boring if it did not provide a welcome distraction. At that point the vehicle was approaching a curve beyond which she could not see, and she braced herself against the lurching that would occur as it went around.

Seated on the box, nursing a twin-barreled ten-gauge Greener shotgun of the pattern made up to the specifications of Wells Fargo, Flint Major also watched the approaching curve. However, his feelings were not the same as those experienced by Betty. Tall, broad-shouldered, and ruggedly good-looking, despite wearing the attire of a cowhand from Texas, he was a guard of considerable experience. He had always considered that one aspect of the curve made it a potentially dangerous area. However, the young easterners who ran the offices had always seen fit to display their supposed superior wisdom by paying no attention to the misgivings of himself or the other guards who rode the route. Admittedly, nothing had ever happened there and he had no reason to believe it would on this occasion, but he preferred to be sure rather than sorry if it did.

"That goddamned tree should've been cut—!" Major growled as he invariably did at the same point in every trip.

"Them college-eddicated know-it-alls back to head office allus reckon to know what's be—!" Joseph "Pizen Joe" Leatherhead responded instinctively without waiting for the comment to be completed.

Both comments came to an end unfinished as each speaker realized the tree in question—taller and somewhat wider around the bole than any others in the vicinity, although this had not made it massive—was no longer standing among the undergrowth. Being dressed in a fashion and with the hairstyle of the old-time Mountain Men, Leatherhead reacted to what he realized could be happening with a speed and precision that might have struck a stranger as being beyond the capability of his obviously advanced years.[4] Even before having gone sufficiently far around the curve to see the tree lying across the trail, he was hauling back on the long leather ribbons and starting to boot home the stagecoach's brake while bellowing in a stentorian voice for the six-horse team to "Whoa!"

Although Major guessed that what he had anticipated might have caused the removal of the tree was about to happen, he was unable to adopt a position of readiness that would allow him to try to circumvent the robbery he was expecting. Such was the excellent condition of the vehicle's brakes—and so excellent was the training to which the team had been subjected—that the deceleration caused him to have to hang on to the side of the seat with one hand while his other grasped the wrist of the shotgun's butt with the intention of preventing it from slipping from his grasp.

From inside the vehicle rose yells of alarm and consternation. However, these were all masculine in timbre, ranging from the bull-like roar from Goodgold through a higher-pitched squeak given by Russel Prouty to a despairing wail redolent of Gilbert Griffin's normally discontented mode of speech, as they were rammed back against the rearward-facing seats taken out of deference for the sex of the fellow traveler. Although as taken aback as the men and in a worse position to suffer the effects of the sudden reduction in speed, Betty gave no vocal protest. Instead, her hands flew up to grasp one of the stout leather straps fastened to the front and rear of the body's interior for such a purpose. Hanging on with all her far-from-inconsiderable strength, she avoided being dislodged.

Before Major could regain control of his movements sufficiently to think of resistance, the matter was taken from his hands.

Wearing their bandannas drawn up to conceal most of their features, Simcock Wilbran and Jack Cunningham—armed respectively with an old Springfield carbine and a no-more-modern ten-gauge shotgun, which the guard considered the more deadly weapon under the circumstances, to supplement their holstered handguns—stood beyond the trunk of the clearly recently felled tree.

"Throw 'em high!" Jesse Wilbran yelled in a voice slightly muffled by his bandanna mask, from where he and Graham Taylor—one of the pair who had not joined in the opening conversation with Libby Craddock at Big Win's—were standing to the right side of the trail with their weapons aimed in a menacing fashion at the stagecoach. "Reach for it, guard, and we'll cut you down!"

"Them's Jesse 'n' Ham don't get, we will!" supplemented Frank Dobson, who was on the other side of the vehicle with the gang's other member, Tom Bower. "And you can count on *that!*"

"Hey, Jack, Sim!" Bower yelled, looking through the window to where Betty was seated. "Belle was right. *She's* here!"

Studying the men ahead with experienced eyes, Major formed an accurate if unflattering assessment of what they were. Effective as it might be at close quarters, a shotgun was a comparatively slow weapon to use and he would be cut down before he got off even one barrel. What was more, should they be provoked into starting to shoot, he felt sure they would do so with indiscriminate disdain for who might become victims. Therefore, he made no attempt to show resistance and allowed the shotgun to remain with the twin barrels pointing toward the floor, although he did not relinquish his hold on the wrist of the butt. He was a competent guard, but it was no part of his duty to carry out something tantamount to committing suicide and would also put in danger the lives of everybody else aboard, including the attractive young woman from Texas for whom he had formed a warm respect and admiration. The latter was the policy of Wells Fargo, and he was in complete agreement with it.

"Throw the scatter down, shotgun," Jesse ordered, glowering at Bower's having spoken before he was able to do so. Gesturing with his right-hand Colt and returning the other to its holster, as he had no proficiency in using it with the left although he would never admit the fact openly, he went on, "Then you both follow it with your belt, hawglegs!"

The order complied with immediately, Leatherhead doing so for the same reason as Major despite seething with controlled rage at the indignity of being treated in such a fashion by what he estimated accurately as being a bunch of stupid kids making out like they were wild, woolly, full-of-fleas and never-curried-below-the-knees genuine owl-hoots. Delighted by the way in which the holdup was going, waiting until they had obeyed his order to climb down on the side away from their discarded weapons, Jesse went to the door of the stagecoach and commanded the occupants to descend without making any fuss.

Watching her fellow travelers despite being surprised by the reference that could only apply to herself and in all probability the lady outlaw, Belle Starr, Betty allowed her right hand to go under the left side of her bolero in a casual-seeming gesture. Remaining seated, knowing he was armed, she turned her gaze first to Goodgold. He was carrying a Tranter revolver in a stiff holster that would effectively prevent anything approaching a fast draw. Therefore, having had considerable experience around guns and gun handlers, she hoped he would not offer any resistance. She had no such concern about the other two. Neither gave any sign of carrying weapons of any kind. Russel Prouty looked flushed, angry, and indignant over the prospect of being robbed. With his face showing even greater misery than previously, Gilbert Griffin seemed to have shrunken into himself while yielding with bad grace to the inevitable.

"My apologies for disturbing you, Miss Hardin, ma'am," Jesse said with exaggerated politeness, having commanded the men to leave the vehicle and moved aside until they did. "But I'd be right obliged happen you'd step out here with the others. Us honest road agents have to make a living."

Puzzled by the mention of her name and certain Belle Starr would not be involved with a holdup in which she herself would be involved, Betty brought her hand from beneath the bolero jacket. Allowing Jesse to take it and refraining from an impulse to take advantage of this action in a way that would have been as painful as it was unexpected, she was assisted in her descent. On being released as soon as she reached the ground, she saw that the driver and guard were standing to one side separate from where the three male passengers formed a dejected, sullen, and dispirited line depending upon which one was studied. From them, she gave the members of the gang within her range of vision a quick and calculating glance. The way the next part of the holdup took place gave her an insight regarding the kind of men who were carrying it out, and she considered the conclusions she drew to be a mixed blessing.

Starting with Goodgold, Jesse took all the not-inconsiderable amount of money and returned the empty wallet to him on the grounds that it might have sentimental value. On Prouty handing over a much thinner wallet, and the bandits showing no sign of being impressed by a warning of personal friendship with the Three Guardsmen, who would leave no stone unturned to bring them to book for their crime, he was compelled by a threat of having it done forcibly and in an embarrassing fashion to surrender the bulky money belt concealed about his waist.

However, a search having established just how little Griffin was carrying, he was not robbed. In fact, being informed that it was not the policy of the gang to take from those who could not afford the loss, he was given a ten-dollar bill taken from the loot acquired from his traveling companions. Having ascertained that the safe-deposit box under the guard's seat was empty, as Leatherhead had claimed, Jesse, with a spluttered profanity for which he immediately apologized to Betty, declared their weapons—being personal property and not that of the Wells Fargo company—would be unloaded but not taken, as was to be the fate of the salesman's Tranter.[5]

Then came the surprise.

"Cut loose 'n' scatter the team, Ben!" Jesse called. "Keep one of 'em, though, so's Miss Hardin can ride it off along of us."

---

1. *A detailed description of how the Abbot & Downing type of stagecoach was constructed and the way in which its passengers and baggage were transported is given in* CALAMITY SPELLS TROUBLE.

2. *The occasion is described in* THE BAD BUNCH.

3. *How Belle Boyd was involved in a scheme that caused various "liberal" groups in a costly and nonproductive venture is told in* CURE THE TEXAS FEVER.

4. *A more complete description of Joseph "Pizen Joe" Leather-*

head, although we did not know his full name at the time of writing and he had a different guard "riding shotgun," is given in the title to which we refer in Footnote 1.

5. A more detailed account of the holdup is given in the volume for which this narrative is an "expansion": Part Two, "The Quartet," THE HALF-BREED.

CHAPTER FOURTEEN

SHE'LL KNOW ALL OF US

"Why should I want to ride off with you?" Betty Hardin queried, although she could guess at the answer, unlikely as she believed it to be.

" 'Cause me 'n' *Belle Starr* allows your folks'll pay plenty to get you back," Jesse Wilbran replied, emphasizing the name because he felt considerable pride in being able to claim he was working with such a famous member of the owlhoot fraternity as the lady outlaw.

"They'll more likely have your hides nailed out to dry to the corral fence," Betty warned, deciding against pointing out the difficulties involved in sending a ransom note and the time that must of necessity elapse before the money demanded for her release would arrive. Furthermore, she was convinced that Belle Starr was not involved in any way with what was contemplated. Not only had the lady outlaw been with Belle Boyd and herself when they were helping bring an end to the career of the murderous Bad Bunch, but the close relationship shared with Mark Counter would preclude any such thing even if being in cahoots with such a bunch of owlhoots was conceivable.[1] "You maybe don't know my grandfather is Ole Devil Hardin, so he'll have his floating outfit hunting for you as soon as he hears what's happened. I've close to a thousand dollars in my handbag and will give you a draft that any bank will accept for another fifteen hundred. Which is more money and less grief than you'll get holding me."

"That is *big* money, Jess!" Simcock Wilbran stated as he and Jack Cunningham advanced from their positions behind the trunk of the fallen tree.

"But not as much as her folks'll hand over to get her back safe, sound 'n' with all her buttons fastened proper," Jesse replied, having briefly given the matter consideration also without wondering how the bank draft could be cashed. He glanced to where Frank Dobson and Thomas Bower had come from the other side of the stagecoach to start unhitching its team with a speed that showed they were well used to handling haulage harness. "Belle sa—I figure he'll not dast take no risks while we've got you, Miss Hardin. I reckon we'll just take our chances on it, so you'd best get ready to mount up 'n' come with us."

"Do you think you can make me?" Betty challenged.

"Hey, now," Cunningham said, swaggering up with his shotgun dangling from his right hand. With the left, he reached forward to grasp the girl's chin to tilt her head back. "Aren't you the spunky li'l—!"

The words were brought to an end by Betty twisting herself free and swinging her knotted right fist with precision and power. Its knuckles, made no less effective by being in a soft black leather riding glove, came around to catch her assailant on the left cheek and stagger him back a couple of steps. Spitting out a profanity, he made as if to lunge forward and she prepared to deal with him in an even more painfully effective fashion. The need did not arise.

"Back off there, damn you, Jack, and keep your talk clean!" Jesse bellowed, swinging his Colt around to give support to his command. "You asked for what you got. No bunch I run don't mishandle nor cuss at no lady." Pausing until his order was obeyed with every evidence of reluctance, he turned his attention back to Betty and continued, "Now, ma'am, here's the way it be. Me 'n' my gang can't go using no violence again' a lady like you, so iffen you don't get on that there hoss 'n' ride with us, I'm going to have these gents cut down one after t'other until you do."

Betty was watching the young man's eyes as he supplied the threat. At different times on the OD Connected she had met most of the top gunfighting men. In their number had been such coldly efficient killers as her cousin, John Wesley Hardin—who had been driven by the evils imposed in the Reconstruction period into being so badly wanted that on his capture even General Hardin's influence in the State could only save him from hanging at the expense of a long term in prison[2]—Ben Thompson, King Fisher, and Clay Allison. Neither Jesse nor any other member of the gang came anywhere close to being in that magic-handed class, but she felt that they were all the more dangerous for it under the circumstances. Probably each of them wanted to acquire the cherished name of "killer" and would not hesitate to shoot down unarmed men if doing so helped them attain the ambition.

Catching the eye of Flint Major, Betty responded to the brief sign he made with an equally close-to-imperceptible shake of her head. The guard was willing to risk his life to save her, as was Pizen Joe Leatherhead, unless she missed her guess. However, she was disinclined to let them take what was almost certainly a suicidal risk. Any attempt was sure to end in bloodshed, and, once started, not one of the men from the stagecoach would be left alive. In her opinion, there was no need for such a thing to happen. Not with Bent's Ford at the most five miles away. By her reckoning, there should be men present there who, collectively or individually, could deal most effectively with two gangs like this one-handed—and left-handed at that. Even if none of Ole Devil's floating outfit had yet arrived, Duke Bent was equally capable of taking measures to effect a rescue.

From the beginning, as she felt sure was the case with the guard and the driver, Betty had studied the gang with eyes that knew the West and could read the signs. Everything she saw suggested they were just youngsters who considered the excitement and money acquired as outlaws preferable to honest hard work. The way in which Jesse was acting implied that he at least had read and was influenced by the luridly fanciful stories such as were given in books like *The True and Factual Life of Jesse and Frank James*. The politeness to her and presentation of money to the poor nester were part of the pattern. In fact, she considered the way in which the leader allowed himself to be called Jesse so openly a desire to make his victims believe he really was the notorious Missouri train and bank robber.

Betty had never met Jesse James, although she had read some of the books that portrayed him as being an unselfish, kindly, and noble Clay County version of Robin Hood using a brace of Colts instead of a yew longbow. On the other hand, she had heard Dusty Fog's views on him both as a reputed hero of the Confederate cause while riding with William Clarke Quantrill's guerrillas and later as an outlaw. They were far from complimentary, but more accurate with regard to his real nature than anything that appeared in print. She could hardly prevent a smile from coming as she remembered her illustrious cousin's reply when one of the younger cowhands at the OD Connected had spoken of "Dingus" James robbing only the rich. "Why sure," Dusty had answered, "Jesse wouldn't rob the poor, they'd have nothing worth taking." Which, she considered, summed up the generous behavior of Jesse James.

There was further proof that the leader of the gang was still trying to copy the fictional Jesse James when Graham Taylor and Sim Wilbran were sent to fetch their horses. On arrival, these proved to be far from the fine and fiery steeds upon which Dingus and his men were claimed to ride. In fact, they looked closer to the culls left behind at some trail-end town as being unworthy of being taken back to Texas. If horses like that had ever been found in the OD Connected's *remuda*, inconceivable as such a thing was with Dusty as *segundo*, all hell would have been raised by Ole Devil and she would have had a few less-than-kind words on the subject to say herself.

"Ham," Jesse said, looking at the horse left from the stagecoach's scattered team. "We can't have no for-real lady like Miss Hardin riding barebacked. She can have your hoss."

While grateful for the thought, the girl would almost have wished to be left with the harness horse, as it looked capable of being able to outrun the mounts of the gang given a chance. Instead of mentioning the point, she allowed herself to be assisted to mount by Jesse and sat getting the feel of the animal, no difficult task for one of her equestrian ability since it was completely docile. With the gang in their saddles, Jesse flipped the noose of his rope around the neck of the animal she was given. She accepted this more as a tribute to her ability as a rider than for any other reason. Such a precaution was hardly due to the quality of the horse she was astride; it was a sorry creature and the worst of the bunch, being unlikely to be able to outrun any of the others.

Not that Betty had any intention of trying to escape. In the unlikely event that she succeeded, the gang might vent their rage by going back and killing the men left with the stagecoach. When she was captured, as she considered almost certain to happen, Jesse could be driven to change his polite treatment as a means of keeping his dominance over the others. If he failed, he would be replaced by the one called Jack, who struck her as being most unlikely to have forgotten the humiliation she had instinctively inflicted and might seek to avenge it in a way she would be compelled to resist even to death. She had already concluded that it would be unwise to take any chances with such a bunch. They would be as dangerous to fool with as a fully loaded and cocked Colt: safe to a certain point, then deadly.

As much to delay the departure, in the hope that something might happen to let the tables be turned upon her captors, as realizing it would come in useful, Betty asked for her overnight bag to be collected from inside the stagecoach. When Jesse inquired whether she wanted any of her other belongings taken, she declined on the truthful grounds that they were all too bulky. With the article she requested and her handbag brought by Sim, but searched and not given to her, the party set off.

WATCHING the gang and their captive ride away, the thoughts of Flint Major and Pizen Joe Leatherhead ran along much the same lines her own had taken. Much as they hated having to let Betty Hardin be abducted without making any attempt to stop its happening, also seeing the bunch as dangerously close to amateurs, they had known better than to try anything. Rather, they concluded they could serve her best by getting to Bent's Ford with the news as quickly as possible. Being left afoot, it would be after dark before they arrived, which meant no pursuit could be started before morning. However, preparations for carrying it out could be made and expert assistance in such matters as following the tracks of the gang obtained, if they were not already available. Spitting disgustedly, the driver followed the guard to gather up their discarded weapons.

"A *fine* thing!" Russel Prouty boomed indignantly, staring after the departing riders. "An armed guard and we still
get robbed with such ease. I'm not without friends among
the Wells Fargo superintendents, my man, and I'll see this
gets reported to them."

"You just do that," Major grunted in an uninterested
fashion. "I reckon they'll be right pleasured to hear I did
like the company says I should when such happens."

"You might even get a bonus for doing her, Flint,"
Leatherhead commented dryly. "Though I wouldn't go
holding my breath a-waiting for it, was I you."

"Why didn't you do *something*?" Prouty demanded, glowering from the old driver to the guard.

"I *did*," Major answered, holstering his Colt after re-
plenishing the chamber with bullets from the loops on his
belt. "That was one *dangerous* bunch there, mister. Happen
I'd tried to fight 'em off, which is against the company's
policy when there's passengers to be considered, they'd likely've killed all of us afore they stopped throwing lead."

"You can practical' guarantee *that*," Leatherhead sup-
ported.

"Jesse!" The portly businessman came much closer to
yelping than speaking in a conversational fashion, directing
his words to the other two passengers, while the driver was
still making the sardonic comment. "They called that outlaw *Jesse*. We've been robbed by Jesse James!"

Although Harold Goodgold had arrived at a similar conclusion, he did not offer to give his support to the theory.
The only two men to be armed were already starting to
walk in the direction of Bent's Ford, and he did not intend
to remain by the stagecoach until they returned with help.
Instead he followed on their heels, and the other passengers, realizing what was portended by the sight, wasted no
time in bringing up the rear.

* * *

ONCE the gang were well clear of the stagecoach trail, Jesse Wilbran drew down the bandanna with which he had masked his face in what he had read was the tradition of owlhoots to avoid being recognized and identified at some future date. Mopping at the sweat that coated his face with his left hand, he gazed at his companions with an air of satisfaction and said everything had gone as planned.

"No point in keeping 'em on, boys," the would-be leader of outlaws declared when none of his companions duplicated his action despite also clearly showing indications of discomfort.

"She'll know all of us without 'em," said Frank Dobson, being an equally avid reader of blood-and-thunder fiction and so just as aware of the reason for wearing such masks. "So we shouldn't let her see our faces."

"We'll be hard put not to, times she'll be with us," Jess stated. "It's going to take a fair piece for us to get paid off, and we can't keep 'em covered all the time until we do. 'Sides which, do you allow as how we're going to let some other bunch get the credit for our job? Like hell we are. Not even Jesse James ever pulled a stage holdup 'n' a kid-snatching—which is what they call what we've done to you, ma'am—one right on top of t'other."

Gripping the reins gently in her black-gloved hands, Betty Hardin managed to hide her smile. It was obvious that Jesse considered there was something very special in what he and his gang had done. Therefore, he was afraid some other outlaw leader might steal his thunder. As she was to learn later, he was annoyed that the early robberies he had committed were barely given a mention in the newspapers. The exploits of the Dalton brothers, Bill Doolin, Sam Bass—the Texas robber of trains and banks—all received far greater coverage. What was more, even Belle Starr, the Rose of Cimarron, and, to a lesser extent, Cattle Annie and Little Britches had received greater attention.[3] However, he was certain that the dual crime he had committed would redress the matter and wanted to be sure that he received all the credit rather than its going somewhere undeserved.

"Hey, Jess," Sim Wilbran remarked after he and the others had also uncovered their faces with equal suggestions of relief. "You reckon Bent'll do what Belle reckons he will when he hears what's happened?"

"Sure," Jesse stated, but he had no intention of allowing the girl to know it had been just the idea of the lady outlaw. "Like we *both* allowed when I let her in with us, he'll telegraph her folks 'n' they'll send word right back for him to pay up 'n' they'll square with him later."

"So that's how you're going to do it," Betty said with what sounded like admiration, having been wondering how the deal would be carried out. She also decided that, whoever the woman might be—and she was still certain it was not Belle Starr—it was obvious who had been the brains behind the affair. "But how do you intend to let Mr. Bent know?"

"That's easy 'nough done," Jesse claimed. "She s— I said as how we'd send her something of your'n like your handbag to prove we'd got you and she could get it 'n' the word to Bent. Which being, you'd best go right now, Sim."

"I'll do it," Jack Cunningham put in truculently, moving his horse forward.

"All right," Jesse assented. Sensing a challenge to his authority and not being ready to take it up right then, he had sufficient low cunning to see how he could effect a compromise without appearing to let himself be compelled to agree. "You can ride along of Sim."

Watching the pair ride away, Betty decided that her task of remaining alive, unmolested and perhaps even effecting an escape, were getting better.

However, having no idea where she was being taken,

the girl concluded that the least she could do in her own behalf was everything she could to help whoever came in search of her find where she was being held.

There was, Betty told herself wryly and not for the first time since her abduction, only herself to blame for her present predicament. Having had to go to Chicago on some business for her grandfather and an aunt—fulfilling a long-held ambition, traveling there by paddle-steamer from Galveston to New Orleans and then by riverboat and train the rest of the way—she had intended to go to Mulrooney in Kansas so that she could at last make the acquaintance of Dusty's wife. She had been in written contact with the beautiful and most efficient titled English lady who had found it necessary to live in the United States under the alias "Freddie Woods" and felt sure they would get along famously.[4]

Unfortunately, a message from the aunt, Selina Blaze—who ran a most successful business as a dressmaker, with clientele spread across the West—which reached Betty in Chicago, had stressed the urgency with which the various latest-mode garments she had acquired in New York and there should be delivered so they could be copied and dispatched to customers. Knowing how much her aunt's livelihood and continued success depended upon such transactions and sensing that any visit with Freddie was sure to be lengthy, she had reluctantly sent a letter to Mulrooney explaining the situation and saying that, as she expected would prove the case from similarly bitter personal experience, her sister-in-law would want to be rid of them. Her cousin and the rest of the floating outfit should be told when she would be passing through Bent's Ford so they could meet her there and she would ensure they behaved themselves properly during the remainder of the journey to the OD Connected.

"Which only goes to prove the way to Hell is paved with

good intentions," Betty mused, as the remainder of the gang started moving while Sim and Cunningham set off in another direction. "Because my intentions were of the *very* best!"

---

1. *How the close relationship between Belle Starr and Mark Counter began, ran its course, and came to an untimely end is recorded in various volumes of the* Floating Outfit *series.*

1a. *The lady outlaw "stars" in her own right—no pun intended—in* WANTED! BELLE STARR.

2. *How John Wesley Hardin was driven to become a wanted man is told in* THE HOODED RIDERS.

3. *Some information regarding the female outlaws given the sobriquets Cattle Annie and Little Britches is given in Part Three, "The Kidnappers,"* TROUBLED RANGE.

4. *Information regarding Freddie Woods is given in various volumes of the* Floating Outfit *series.*

4a. *She also makes "guest" appearances under her married name, Mrs. Freddie Fog, in* NO FINGER ON THE TRIGGER *and* CURE THE TEXAS FEVER.

CHAPTER FIFTEEN

SHE PAID A HELL OF A
PRICE FOR DOING IT

"Howdy, Miss Starr," Simcock Wilbran greeted, having received no encouragement when he had addressed the reddish-brunette as "Belle" during their previous meeting. "It went off slick 'n' easy as you said it would."

Having spent the intervening time at Big Win's place without incident, other than its owner—having been told by the bartender what happened in her absence—demanding to be paid for being allowed to stay and not be required to carry on the pose of being a saloon girl, Libby Craddock had been waiting in the woodland a short distance from it at the place she had arranged as a rendezvous for herself and whichever of the gang came to let her know how the holdup and kidnapping went off. Despite having had no intention of going on with their association, or staying in the West once she got her hands on the currency-printing plates, she had pretended there would be other and even more lucrative robberies in which they could participate. Therefore, she had not doubted they would come to bring her share of the loot.

"Where are her bags?" the reddish-brunette demanded coldly, having stipulated that these items should be taken with the woman she believed to be Belle Boyd, looking pointedly at the saddles of the pair's horses. "I said for you to bring them."

"Hell, there was a big pile of 'em on top of the stage," Jack Cunningham growled, feeling resentment over having a woman speak to him in such a bossy fashion even if she was—as he, like all the others, believed to be—the famous Belle Starr. "Big 'n's to boot. We wasn't going to hang around going through 'em all, nor sorting her'n out to weigh the hosses down toting 'em along when they likely wouldn't have nothing but women's doodads in 'em."

"Did she ask you to take *any* of them?" Libby snarled.

"Naw," Sim replied in a placating tone, deciding against mentioning that nobody had remembered until too late that the "lady outlaw" had said they should fetch all their victim's baggage and pleased Cunningham had been sufficiently quick-witted to come up with a passable reason to explain the failure to do so. "But Jess allowed she should have her handbag and the little 'n' that was inside the coach 'cause it'd got things she'd need while we was holding her for ransom. We got us a fair amount of cash money out of the handbag, so we've added your share of it to what we got from the three fellers. It comes to a tidy sum."

"Wasn't there *anything* else in either of them?" the reddish-brunette inquired, deciding she had better change her attitude, as she could see Cunningham was showing signs of annoyance over her behavior and sensing he could be dangerous if crossed. Wanting to avoid arousing suspicions and having no intention of saying what she was really interested in hearing about, she went on, "I mean like jewelry."

"Was some in the handbag," Sim admitted. "But Jess said as how she was to be let keep it, seeing's how we'd get a better'n fair price as ransom from her folks and it wouldn't be right to go robbing no lady when such wasn't our intention for taking her with us."

"And what about in the other bag?" Libby queried, concluding that Jesse Wilbran would think in such a fashion to keep up his pretense of being a noble and gallant outlaw in the mold of the fictional Jesse James.

"Just ordinary she-male's doodads," the younger Wilbran brother replied with something like a blush coming to his cheeks. "You know, like the kind you see in the dream-books iffen you get to one afore your momma's tore 'em out."

"There wouldn't have been some flat lead plates about this size?" the reddish-brunette said, trying to make the words sound casual. While gesturing the appropriate dimensions with her hands, she hoped that if the answer was in the affirmative none of her dupes had noticed and drawn the correct conclusions from the way the items were inscribed. "Women often carry them for—well, *men* who've been around as much as you don't need telling what for."

"Ain't never seen no woman toting such," Sim admitted, trying to sound worldly-wise. "And Miss Hardin for sure wasn't."

"Oh well, they wouldn't have been worth taking anyway," Libby said, needing to exert all her willpower to speak as if the subject were of no great consequence. Deciding that the only consolation she could draw was that her share of the loot would be a welcome addition to her depleted revenue, she continued, "Tell Jesse and the others I'll leave word with Big Win where we can get together for our next job."

"Aren't you coming back with us?" Sim asked, seeing that a horse with a fair-size bedroll strapped to the cantle of its saddle was standing hitched to a bush.

"No!" Libby replied, and realized she had spoken with too much vehemence, so sought to make amends as she had no wish to stir up suspicion. "I've got to go and pick up some information for another job we can pull, but I'll come back to Big Win's to collect my cut of the ransom money when it gets here."

"We might as well get going, then, Sim," Cunningham stated, showing relief for some reason, which the reddish-brunette could not understand but decided against questioning. "We've got things to do."

"Jess'll let you know when your cut's come, ma'am," Sim promised, doffing his hat and then following his companion's example by mounting his horse to ride away.

"I should live so long," Libby said disdainfully but sotto voce. She was relieved that neither of the men had had sufficient intelligence to give any thought to how she would learn of the ransom money's arrival. "Seeing as Boyd hadn't got the plates with her, they must be in her bags on the coach," she continued to herself. "So, if they're left at Bent's Ford like they were supposed to be, I might find a way to get them tonight."

"BUT what is there to *ford*?"

The question had been asked on many occasions by people seeing Bent's Ford for the first time.[1]

Having made many visits, the Ysabel Kid was not surprised by what he saw shortly after nightfall. Finding there were no vacant stalls in the stable and being aware of how his big white stallion never took kindly to having strange members of its kind in close proximity, he attended to its needs and left it in a small unoccupied corral. There was sufficient light from the moon for anybody else who came along to see it, and he assumed they would have sufficient knowledge of equestrian matters to draw the necessary conclusions and not offer to place their own animals in with it. Satisfied that Nigger would have everything needed for a restful night, he toted his saddle and bedroll with him to the main building.

On entering the barroom of the main building, the Kid found himself greeted with an extra warmth by the owner and told there was a serious problem at hand. Big, burly, jovial-looking, Duke Bent had more the appearance of a working cowhand than the very wealthy and successful businessman he had become since establishing his place. One of his chief pleasures in life was to sing as bass in a quartet, and, as there was nothing else of importance demanding his attention—the fact that the expected stagecoach had not yet arrived arousing no concern, as not even Pizen Joe Leatherhead could adhere to the timetable set out by the Wells Fargo supervisor for the region—he was hoping to indulge in it.

"I've got Chris here, and now you, as tenors," Bent declared with a note of asperity in his Texas drawl, after having one of his male employees take charge of the Kid's belongings. "But damned if I can find me a baritone around. Could've used Mark, seeing's how we can't get a better'n. Where's he at, Lon?"

"Him 'n' Dusty had to stay on to Mulrooney for a spell," the Kid answered, trying not to look too discomfited by the reminder of how he had deserted his two *amigos*. Wanting to change the subject, he looked at the man by Bent's side. "Howdy, Chris. Billy said you was out Muskogee way when we met up."

"Was," United States Deputy Marshal Chris Madsen replied. Tall and lithe, he had brown hair, was moderately good-looking, and had a neatly trimmed mustache. He wore the clothing of a working cowhand, with his badge of office fastened to the left side of his calfskin vest, and had an ivory-handled Colt Cavalry Model Peacemaker in the fast-draw holster of his gunbelt. "But good ole Bill Doolin wasn't, so I reckoned I'd come to give Duke some trade afore I went hunting him someplace else. Damn it, Kid, I was looking forward to getting into a quartet myself."

"Well, I'll be damned!" the black-dressed Texan exclaimed, glancing toward the front entrance as the batwing doors were pushed open. "Could be we've got ourselves the baritone we want."

"You reckon so, huh?" Madsen inquired, studying the newcomer with considerable if not overnoticeable interest.

Having halted when just across the threshold, as if wanting to let his eyes become accustomed to the increase in light, the subject of the comment and question was just over medium height, stocky, and had a tanned face with a cheerful expression. Pushed to the back of his head, his white Stetson brought crinkly black hair into view, and more of it could be seen under the open neck of his shirt. His clothing was in the same somewhat dandified and yet totally functional style for which Mark Counter was famous. However, while he looked like a Texan who was tophand with cattle, his well-designed and -crafted gunbelt and its rosewood-handled Colt Artillery Model Peacemaker were those of one very well versed in their use.

"Howdy, Lon, how're you?" the newcomer greeted, advancing with a broad grin on his face and his right hand outstretched. "Ain't seen you in a coon's age. Hey, though, I saw ole Nigger out to the corral all on his lonesome and'd've sneaked a stud from him was the time right. Where at's Dusty 'n' Mark?"

"Feeling fit as a flea," the Kid replied to the first question, shaking hands and wishing to hell that everybody would stop reminding him of what he had done to his two best friends in all the world. "You couldn't've come at a better time——!"

"Why, sure," the man drawled. "I figured to drop by for a game of poker. Yes sir, sure as my name's *Eph Tenor*, I feel lucky tonight."

"Can't oblige you with poker, *Eph*," Bent apologized, laying a similar emphasis on the name. "But we're looking for a baritone to sing some quartet with us. You want in on it?"

"Why, sure," agreed the man who introduced himself as Eph Tenor, his voice and expression indicating that he, too, was a keen advocate of such a diversion. "Who-all's singing the other tenor?"

"Allow you two's never met afore," Bent drawled. "This here's Chris Madsen, Eph. Chris, get acquainted with Eph Tenor from Texas."

"Pleased to meet you, Chris," Tenor declared, his grin never wavering as he held out his right hand.

"Likewise," Madsen responded in just as amiable a fashion. "You up this way on business, Eph?"

"*Me?*" Tenor said, sounding shocked in an amused way. "Nope. I've got me a li'l Denton mare out there's can run a quarter of a mile faster'n most hosses, even Lon's Nigger, can cover a hundred yards."

"Any particular town in mind for running her?" the deputy marshal inquired in the same seemingly uninterested fashion.

"Nope," Tenor replied. "Just looking around for any place where I can find suckers's reckon they've got something to beat li'l ole Denton."

"Well, you won't get any in here tonight," Bent declared. "So take something to wash the dust out of your throat and let's get us to doing some quarteting."

There were only a few customers in the barroom, the horses occupying the stalls having been put there by a man taking them for sale in one of the larger Indian Nation towns and wanting to ensure that they arrived in the best possible condition. However, as the quartet singing sessions at the Ford had acquired a reputation for excellence, they and the half-dozen saloon girls who were present formed an attentive and enthusiastic audience. Nor, while it was not up to professional standards, was the singing unworthy of the reception it was accorded, even though only the Kid and Bent had previously performed together.

At the request of the other three, Madsen opened the concert with his rendering of "Little Joe the Wrangler." As U.S. Deputy Marshal Billy Tilghman had claimed, he had a good, if untrained, tenor and received quite adequate support from the other three. The same applied when the Kid took the lead with the sad story of "My Darling Clementine." Then, regardless of the name he had given, Tenor demonstrated that he was a better-than-fair baritone and produced a few sniffles from a couple of sentimental girls with his rendition of "Oh Bury Me Not On the Lone Prairie." Each entry was greeted with applause from the audience, and after a pause for liquid refreshment Bent's thunderous bass gave out with "The Cowman's Prayer" and evoked more tears from the same source.

The owner of the Ford was just concluding with "But I've had my say, and now amen!" when the batwing doors were thrust open and all thoughts of music came to an abrupt end.

As he had not heard any indications of the stagecoach's arrival, Bent realized that something was seriously amiss when he saw who was about to enter the barroom.

Arriving at the same conclusion, the other members of the quartet accompanied their bass singer as he started to walk forward.

"Sorry to come a-busting in on your quarteterizing, Duke, young ladies 'n' gents," Pizen Joe Leatherhead apologized, leading the other men into the building. "Only, we run into a smidgen of fuss back a ways."

"A *smidgen!*" Russel Prouty almost howled, limping by the elderly driver and showing far more signs of dishevelment as a result of the exercise he had been compelled to take in walking from the scene of the holdup. "We've been waylaid and robbed, damn it!"

"Don't end it there," Leatherhead suggested, looking at the approaching black-dressed Texan in something close to trepidation and not relishing the information he must give. "They took Miss Hardin with 'em, Kid."

"She's Ole Devil Hardin's granddaughter!" Harold Goodgold announced, lacking the driver's knowledge and wanting to show off his own. "All hell's going to break over what's happened."

"Mister," the Kid growled, his voice and demeanor becoming like that of a Pehnane Comanche Dog Soldier about to swear his lodge oath of vengeance. "Said hell's going to break loose a damned sight sooner's you reckon. What happened?"

"It was the James gang!" Prouty asserted, and despite the claims he had made regarding their close acquaintance, he did not appear to recognize Madsen or even notice the badge of office. "Damn it, I consid—!"

"The *James* gang?" the deputy marshal asked, having been looking at Tenor in a speculative fashion. "Are you *sure* of that?"

"I am, sir," the pompous businessman declared. "Oh, you're a—!"

"The leader was a real big man," Goodgold interrupted eagerly, not wanting to be left out of the limelight. "Six foot three or four at least, and mean-looking."

"Weren't they masked?" Madsen queried, and, noticing Tenor was starting to put his hat on, said in a quiet yet authoritative tone, "Don't go just yet, Eph. We've some more quartet singing to do when I've 'tended to this."

"Of course they were masked!" Prouty snapped, determined to remain as the center of attention. "You should have seen him, it couldn't have been anybody except Jesse James. Big, at least six foot four, and his black eyes were the coldest I've ever seen. They seemed to look clear through you."

"And you're both *sure* it was Jesse James?" the deputy marshal asked after another speculative glance in Tenor's direction.

"One of them even called him Jesse," the salesman declared. "There were at least ten in the gang, and we daren't make a fight, having Miss Hardin along."

"That was real good of you," the Kid said dryly, considering that Betty would have been better able to hold up her end in a fight than either of the men.

"You gents'd best come on over to the bar and take something," Bent offered, knowing Madsen—who was growing increasingly exasperated, although only a person who knew him well would have known—wanted to deal with Leatherhead and Flint Major rather than with either of the pair who had been doing the talking. "Leave the driver and guard to handle things, it being their chore."

Giving the pair no chance to debate the matter, the owner of the Ford deftly ushered them and Gilbert Griffin away from the rest of the party. With them gone, Madsen was told what had happened and obtained a more accurate description of the leading perpetrator. He was also supplied with a correct assessment of the gang's ability, and he drew some consolation from suspecting the pose of the leader being that of a noble and gallant outlaw would keep Betty safe from molestation until at least after the attempt at arranging a ransom was made. The trouble was, he had said, nothing could be done about trying to hunt them down until daybreak, as not even the Kid was able to follow tracks under the prevailing conditions regardless of the moonlight.

RETURNING from the backhouse after having gone to "answer the call of nature," the Ysabel Kid needed to keep calling upon all the stoical nature he had acquired during his upbringing as a Pehnane to curb his desire for setting

out to locate and rescue Betty Hardin. While he realized
he could not accomplish anything before daylight, it was
hard to just wait around for the time to come. He appre-
ciated that Duke Bent's insistence in continuing with the
quartet singing had helped in that direction.

However, having fulfilled the need to relieve himself of
the beer drunk with which all the quartet were supplied
by members of their enthusiastic audience to help keep
the vocal cords operating smoothly, the Kid was ready to
do more singing. As he glanced instinctively toward the
corral in which his big white stallion was standing,
something in its demeanor attracted his attention. Turning
his gaze in the direction it was looking in the alert fashion
he knew so well, he saw a flicker of light inside the small
and stoutly constructed wooden building he knew had a
sign reading, "WELLS FARGO. PRIVATE." Being aware
that it was used to store baggage or other property that was
being held for some reason by Bent in the capacity of station agent, he knew that it should not be open at that hour
of the night.

Taken with the behavior of the horse, which he had
trained to perform the kind of sentry duties a Pehnane
tehnep expected to be carried out by a favorite war pony,
the Kid concluded that the matter required investigation.[2] Drawing and cocking his Colt Dragoon without the
need for conscious thought, knowing instinctively it might
serve his purposes better than the bowie knife under the
circumstances, he advanced with the stealth of a stalking
cougar.

AFTER parting company with Simcock Wilbran and
Jack Cunningham, Libby Craddock had decided upon
what she should do next. Because it had not been mentioned when Jesse Wilbran was telling her how he was
intending to carry out the holdup of the stagecoach, nor

while she was talking to the pair who brought her portion of the loot, she was unaware of the team's having been turned loose. Therefore, she assumed the baggage she believed belonged to Belle Boyd would have been delivered to Bent's Ford along with the news of what had taken place.

Wondering what would happen next, the reddish-brunette had reassumed the rest of her masculine disguise—having donned only the clothing for the interview, as she considered nothing more was required since she was still believed to be Belle Starr—and returned to Big Win's place. Being fortunate enough to find the bartender alone, she had told him that she was going to come into possession of some valuable stolen paintings and wanted to keep them somewhere safe while she went to make a deal for their disposal to a wealthy local businessman. Her expression when he had suggested she leave them with Big Win had drawn a wry and knowing grin before he suggested she deposit them in Wells Fargo's storehouse at Bent's Ford, where they would be kept under lock and key. Learning all she could about the place, she had felt certain she could achieve her purpose of obtaining the currency-printing plates by going there.

Arriving after having left her horse in concealment some distance away, wanting to avoid any chance of arousing unwanted attention by riding up and then not entering the main building, she advanced on foot. Going by the small corral, she had heard its solitary occupant giving a snort. Although the magnificent white horse was staring at her and tossing its head, it made no attempt to approach from where it stood in the center of the enclosure. Without noticing its sex, she saw it was an animal of excellent quality and decided she would help herself to it on having carried out the search and, she hoped, found what she was looking for.

Having had much experience at riding in one of her acts with the Circus Maximus, Libby was confident she could handle it with sufficient ease to carry out the theft. Nor, she was equally sure, would she find any difficulty in finding a buyer for such a fine beast, and the money it brought in would make a welcome addition to the sum already in her possession. Unless anything unexpected should happen, she would have enough to let her look around for someone willing to pay more than Lachlan Lachlan of the McLachlans for the plates.

Reaching the building without anything suggesting she had been detected as a result of the horse's behavior, the reddish-brunette did not need to open the front of the small bull's-eye lantern she was carrying lit in her left hand to pick the massive padlock. However, once inside, she illuminated the contents of the room with its light. After examining each in turn, she realized with a growing anger that the baggage she was seeking was not present. Snapping the front of the lamp closed, she returned to the door.

On emerging, Libby found herself confronted by a tall and slender young man clad all in black and holding a big revolver in his right hand. While taken aback for a moment, she was pleased she had followed the habit acquired when carrying out robberies unaided by male companions in the East. After leaving Big Win's, she had taken off the masculine aids other than the clothing. Leaving her Stetson and loose-fitting jacket with her horse, she had drawn the shirt as tightly as she could and opened its front to a level that, as she wore nothing underneath, left no doubt that she was a woman. On previous occasions when she had been caught in the act, doing so had given her an element of surprise that enabled her to deal with the man who did so.

For once in his life, the Ysabel Kid was taken by surprise. Instead of the man he had anticipated, he found the intruder he was looking at to be a woman. Although it had been said the gang made it appear they were working with Belle Starr, neither he nor any of the others had believed this was true. Not only would she refuse to participate in the kidnapping of Betty Hardin, she would never have become involved with the kind of outlaws the driver and guard of the stagecoach had assessed them to be. Therefore, it had never occurred to him that a woman might be involved with them, much less be making an attempt to rob the Wells Fargo storehouse. What was more, while armed, she was not holding a weapon.

Letting the lantern fall, Libby made ready to take advantage of the hesitancy being shown by the Texan. Realizing her waistbelt was drawn tight to hold the shirt in the desired position, she did not attempt to reach for the Smith & Wesson revolver tucked into it. Instead, she darted forward and sent her right foot into the air with the kind of precision she had demonstrated when kicking open the French windows of Countess Olga Simonouski's suite at the Grand Republic Hotel in Washington, D.C. What was more, her aim was good enough to achieve her purpose.

Caught under the jaw with considerable force, the Kid's head snapped back and he pitched over with bright lights erupting in his skull.

However, as the Texan was going down, his forefinger instinctively tightened on the trigger of the Dragoon and it went off thunderously.

"And I know what Betty Hardin 'n' Belle Boyd can do with their feet!" was the Kid's last conscious thought as he sprawled supine on the ground. "I'll *never* hear the end of this."

Although the bullet flew harmlessly across the open range, the reddish-brunette knew the noise of the detonation would be heard in the main building and was certain to bring men to investigate the cause. Even as the thought came, she heard shouts and saw some of them coming through the front entrance. She realized she would stand a good chance of being caught, or perhaps even shot, before she could reach where she had left her horse. However, she remembered there was another and better means of escape closer at hand. It was one, moreover, she had intended to take in any case. With that thought in mind, she ran toward the small corral and ducked between two of its rails.

For all the skill she had acquired in riding, the reddish-brunette now failed to take two things into account. Every horse she had worked with was either a mare or a gelding that had been broken to accept handling by strangers. Even worse from her point of view was that the big white stallion would allow only a very few people other than its master to even approach in safety. The knowledge came too late. As she was walking forward, the huge animal gave vent to a fighting scream and presented a sight so terrifying as it rushed toward her that she was numbed into immobility. Nor was she granted even a moment to recover from the shock before she was sent sprawling and the metal-shod hooves of her attacker began to smash home with all the terrible force of a powerful body behind them.

"Don't you do *that*, not for no lousy hoss thief, Chris!" Pizen Joe Leatherhead warned, as the deputy marshal was about to enter into the corral. "There's only the Kid could stop Nigger right now!"

"And he's in no shape to do it!" Eph Tenor went on, hurrying to where the black-dressed Texan was starting to show signs of regaining consciousness.

"I don't know who she was, nor what she was after in the store there," the Kid said after he had been revived by a drink of whiskey and calmed down his stallion sufficiently to allow the gory remains of the dead woman to be removed. He spoke with some discomfort, but was thankful to have escaped without sustaining a broken jaw. "But she paid a hell of a price for doing it."

"Yeah," drawled the unsentimental old driver. "And she's surely stopped there being any more quartet singing tonight, 'less'n you fellers want me to take over from young Lon here."

---

1. *How the name of Bent's Ford came into being and the legends about it were produced is told in Part Two, "The Quartet,"* THE HALF-BREED.

2. Tehnep: *an experienced and seasoned Comanche warrior.*

CHAPTER SIXTEEN

TROUBLE BEING, I WON'T BE HERE

"Howdy, Win," United States Deputy Marshal Chris Madsen greeted as he and the Ysabel Kid walked up to the bar of the fat woman's place of business. He swung a gaze around the room, noticing that several of the men present were trying to look as if unconcerned by his arrival. "Lordy Lord, happen the Devil dropped his net in here, he'd come up with a swell catch."

After the body of Libby Craddock had been removed from the corral, a task performed by Pizen Joe Leatherhead and another grizzled old-timer because none of the younger men were willing to handle such a gruesome object as what remained of her, a search had been instigated for the means by which she had arrived. Her horse was located without too much difficulty and was brought back to Bent's Ford. While the bedroll strapped to the saddle contained a number of items that the peace officer found of considerable interest, there was nothing to inform him of her identity. However, he concluded that she might have been the woman whom the gang who kidnapped Betty Hardin had suggested they believed was Belle Starr. The Kid and Duke Bent had stated that the corpse definitely was not that of the lady outlaw, nor had the deputy marshal—tactfully refraining from asking the latter where he had made her acquaintance—believed it would be.

At dawn that morning, while Leatherhead and Flint Major took a fresh team of horses to collect the stagecoach and the means to remove the felled tree from the trail, the search for Betty and her captors was commenced. Madsen took the Kid, and Eph Tenor agreed without argument or hesitation when he was asked by the peace officer to accompany them. Putting to use his considerable experience at reading sign, which Madsen would willingly have admitted if asked was the best to come his way, the Kid had at first found no difficulty in following the line taken by the departing gang. What was more, with the aid of pieces of hair he had found, he was able to say the color of some of the horses being used by the gang.

However, despite the opinion of the driver and guard that they had only recently become owlhoots, Jesse Wilbran and his cohorts had soon proved to know quite a bit about concealing signs of their passage. Helped by the gloves and a handkerchief that the girl had contrived to leave at points where such an indication was most welcome, the three men kept going until a fall of rain coincided with an area of rocky terrain to render all evidence of the route being taken by the gang unfindable. Nor, if Betty had managed to leave any clues, could these be discovered despite a rigorous search.

Shortly after noon, Madsen had suggested they go to see Big Win. As Libby Craddock had been informed, her place was notorious as a gathering place for outlaws and little of a criminal nature happened in Oklahoma that she did not get to hear about sooner or later. Setting off in the required direction, they had all hoped it would prove sooner than later on this occasion. Just before they had come into sight of the big building, pointing out that he was less likely to be identified by whoever was inside,

Tenor had suggested he go ahead and waited for his companions inside the barroom. This had been agreed upon, so the Kid and Madsen had given him about twenty minutes' start on them.

The time spent in allowing Tenor his period of grace was not wasted.

Leaving their horses on the edge of the woodland, the Kid and the deputy marshal walked over to examine the animals standing hitched in front of the big wooden building.

"Could be we've hit pay dirt, Chris," the black-dressed Texan stated, looking at two of the horses with some care, and to somebody who had come to know him as well as the peace officer had, there was a sense of satisfaction in his voice. "A washy bay 'n' a blue-roan."

"Don't know how it is down to Texas," Madsen answered, despite believing his companion had something specific to work on and was not merely indulging in idle or sensation-seeking guesswork. "But we're sort of up to our assholes in washy bays 'n' blue-roans all through the Indian Nation."

"Likely us Texans leave off a whole slew of our culls passing through," the Kid countered. "Only this washy bay's favoring its off hind a mite like the one we was after until two of 'em split and took it with 'em. Anyways, I'm willing to put up money's says they're two of the sons of bitches we're after. You want to take me for a ten spot, Chris?"

"Why not?" the peace officer said with a grin.

The way Madsen saw it, he could not lose on the deal. If the Kid was wrong, he would be ten dollars better off. On the other hand, should the conclusion prove correct, it would be worth the money to lay hands on two members of the gang. With this done, he felt sure they could be induced in some way to tell where the remainder were to be located.

Without another word, the black-dressed Texan went to the other side of the bay and removed something from where it had been dangling concealed. Letting out a grunt of annoyance mingled with satisfaction, the peace officer saw he was being shown a woman's overnight bag. It was made of excellent-quality black leather and on the side were two sets of initials in silver: *BH* and *OD*, the *O* touching the straight side of the *D*.

"Damn it, Lon," Madsen growled in mock exasperation. "I've been slickered. You saw this damned thing!"

"And *you* didn't," the Kid replied, holding out his right hand palm up.

"I'll pay you as soon as we're through here."

"Nope, Grandpappy Long Walker allus used to tell me, 'Keep bow strung, keep knife sharp, make everybody pay off their gambling debts right pronto.'"

"I'm damned if I know how that Dutch jasper ever slickered you blasted redsticks out'n Manhattan Island for the price he give."

"Or me," the Kid admitted, returning the traveling bag to where it had come from before accepting the two five-dollar pieces he was being offered. "Only, we're fixing on getting it back for the same's we got, and with something else to boot. What say we go on in and get her done?"

"I thought you'd *never* get around to asking," Madsen declared. "Shall I lead?"

"I wouldn't have it no other way," the Kid asserted cheerfully. "Happen they start shooting at you, don't fall down and let 'em hit me accidental."

On entering the barroom, the Kid and Madsen had found several men were either sitting around in groups or lounging by the counter. Clearly having done what he considered was making the most of his time, their companion was occupying a table against the right-side walk and appeared to be making himself pleasant to the best-looking pair of girls present.

"I don't know what you mean, Mr. Madsen," Big Win said without any suggestion or malice. "So far's I *know*, everybody here's a honest 'n' hardworking feller."

"Aren't *all* your customers honest 'n' hardworking fellers?" the deputy marshal said dryly, resuming his scrutiny of the room's occupants.

Even as Madsen did so, much to his amazement, he saw Tenor suddenly rise from the table. Showing he could utilize the potential of his holster to its full advantage, the stocky Texan brought out his Colt Civilian Model Peacemaker and seemed to be aiming its four-and-three-quarter-inches barrel toward the peace officer. Even as Madsen commenced his own draw, he knew he could not complete it swiftly enough to prevent the shorter revolver from being fired.

The calculation proved correct. However, Madsen discovered he was not the target selected. Swinging a short distance onward, the gun held by Tenor roared. Hearing the sound of the close-passing bullet striking what could only be human flesh and almost certainly in the chest, followed by something metallic falling to the floor and the crash of another shot, the peace officer allowed his Colt to slide back into leather and turned his gaze in the appropriate direction. Feeling grateful that he had not completed his draw and fired, Madsen's gaze came to rest on a burly and unshaven man in unclean range clothes who had obviously just come in. Clasping both hands to his left breast, he stumbled back and crashed supine.

"I'll 'tend to it, Chris," the Kid offered, drawing his old Dragoon Colt as a basic precaution and walking across to look at the victim of Tenor's marksmanship. One glance told him all he needed to know. Replacing the heavy old revolver, he stepped back and, spreading his hands palms outward at waist level in a gesture everybody present recognized for what it meant, he announced, "He's cashed, dead as a six-day stunk-up skunk."

"Sorry I didn't get a chance to say what I was aiming to do, *Marshal,*" Tenor said, spinning the revolver deftly on his trigger finger before returning it to the holster. "Only me 'n' him's never been what you might call close *amigos.* Fact, you might even say we was enemies and I concluded he was looking for evens."

"I'd say you got 'em," Madsen answered, hiding his amusement over the way in which the stocky Texan had prevented their association from being deduced. Turning his gaze to the massive woman beyond the counter, he went on, "Looks like *one* of your fellers isn't so honest 'n' hardworking's he likely told you he was, Win."

Far from being after Tenor, the peace officer knew the dead man had been known only as Dutch Charlie and had been kicked out of Bill Doolin's gang for being too brutal and was wanted for two cold-blooded murders he was known to have committed. He had sworn he would kill all the Three Guardsmen for making him one of their prime targets, and, having seen Madsen, was clearly intending to make a start at it. What was more, as his presence had not been detected by the peace officer—who was concentrating upon Big Win—he might easily have succeeded but for the intervention of the stocky Texan.

"I don't know *everybody* as comes in, Mr. Madsen, how could I?" the woman answered. "Fact being, I've never even saw him afore."

"Would you know anything about whoever it was robbed the stagecoach to Bent's yesterday?" the peace officer inquired, having signaled for the woman to move to the end of the counter and held down his voice to a level only she and the black-dressed Texan who had accompanied them could hear.

"They did more'n just rob it," the Kid supplemented, his face suddenly taking on the appearance of an annoyed Pehnane dog soldier. "They lit off with General Hardin's granddaughter, Betty."

"Gen—!" Big Win began, and it was clearly taking all her willpower to avoid speaking louder than the two men had. "*Ole Devil* Hardin?"

"That's just who he is," the black-dressed Texan confirmed. "Which I threw my bedroll in the OD Connected's chuck wagon way back."

"I know who *you* are," the woman declared, and she looked uneasy. "But honest to God, Kid, Marshal, I didn't know nothing about *that*."

"I'd be willing to bet you could make a right good stab at saying who does," Madsen stated. "Just have a try, *please*."

"I'll make it *pretty please*," the Kid went on, but the seemingly polite words came out as a threat.

"Try that pair of young'n's over there," Big Win suggested, jerking a thumb to where Simcock Wilbran and Jack Cunningham were sitting at a table holding glasses of beer. "They was in with four more day afore yesterday and got talking some with a fancy eastern gal who was making out to be a saloon floozy looking for work. Don't know what was said, having been away all afternoon, but Wilf, my bardog, allows they might've been talking about doing a holdup. Gal's not here anymore."

"We know," the Kid drawled. "She'd got real taking ways. Trouble being, she tried to take ole Nigger."

"May the Good Lord have mercy on her soul," Win intoned, and crossed herself. "Anyways, that pair was close to the blanket last time, 'cording to Wilf. Only, they're not today. Each of 'em bought their beers with a ten-dollar bill 'n' pulled it off a roll."

"Let's go have a word with 'em, Lon," Madsen suggested, then looked hard at the Indian-dark Texan. "And a *word's* all I mean. We need them alive to do some talking."

"I'll mind it," the Kid said with a grin that held no mirth. "But happen any one of 'em's laid hands on Betty, I'll—!"

"And I'll help you," the peace officer asserted grimly. "Let's get her done."

Walking toward where Wilbran and Cunningham sat staring at them in the fascinated way of a rabbit faced by a weasel, the Kid studied them. He formed an accurate if far-from-flattering assessment of their abilities. Unless he was sadly wrong, taking them would prove easy enough. Once that was done, should he be given the cooperation promised by the peace officer—which he did not doubt would prove the case—he was confident they could be induced to tell him all he needed to know.

Every eye in the room was focused on the Kid and Madsen as they walked slowly across the room. That particularly applied to Wilbran and, although made of somewhat sterner material, Cunningham. Both were staring most at the silver badge of officer on the deputy marshal's vest, and the beer they had consumed seemed to have turned to ice in their stomach. For his part, Madsen was studying them with an equal care. His instincts as a peace officer suggested that, even if not the pair he and the Kid hoped they would be, they had guilty knowledge about something else. Therefore, he was alert and kept his right hand hanging close to the butt of his Colt, ready to fetch it out at the first indication that it might be needed.

"You boys done much riding?" Madsen asked as he came to a halt with the Kid to his left side.

"Who wants to know?" Cunningham asked, making a far-from-successful attempt to sound tougher than he was feeling.

"I do, for one," the Kid asserted in his most mean tone, which meant he was *very* frightening to the pair of young outlaws. "So don't hand us any bull droppings, you sons of bitches. That gal you thought was Belle Starr told us all we need to know about you."

"She sold us out, Jack!" Wilbran screeched.

"You stupid bast—!" Cunningham began, starting to thrust back his chair.

The movement ended half completed as the Kid, moving with the speed of the Pehnane dog soldier he had been so well trained to be, lunged forward. However, it was not the Dragoon Colt he brought out. Coming from its sheath, the massive blade of the bowie knife went so its point was pricking Cunningham's chin. Acting with a similar speed, Madsen brought out his Colt. Although its ostensible purpose was to cover Wilbran, he was ready to use it to quell any opposition that might come from elsewhere in the room.

"These two stinking, no-account sons of bitches've helped take off with *Ole Devil Hardin's* granddaughter, gents," the black-dressed Texan announced as Cunningham sank back onto the chair and sat as if turned to stone. "Which, in case some of you don't know it already, I'm the Ysabel Kid."

"You do what you want with them, Mr. Madsen, Kid!" Big Win boomed. "Nobody's wants to stay my *friend'll* stop you."

"Where at's your hideout?" the Kid asked, keeping his knife in position and knowing that—in addition to his having made it plain where he stood on the issue—there would be no intervention from the other men in the room, even though they were almost certainly all outlaws after the warning that had been given.

"What's in it for us, happen we talk?" Cunningham croaked.

"I'll tell you what's in it for you, happen you *don't*," the Kid replied, and the clip joint of the bowie sank in just deep enough to start a trickle of blood flowing down the outlaw's neck. "I'm going to take you out 'n' see if some of the things I learned from my grandpappy, Chief Long Walker of the Comanche, can make you change your minds."

"Y-you can't let him *torture* us, Marshal!" Wilbran wailed.

"That's the living truth," the peace officer admitted. "And I wouldn't let it be done. Trouble being, I won't be here to stop it."

"Aw hell, Marshal," the Kid drawled. "Ain't no call for you to leave. I'll just take 'em off one at a time into the piney woods out there 'n' work where you can't see 'em. Hey, though, did any of you fellers ever see how a Comanch' does things like I'm aiming to?"

"I've seed how Kiowa do it," Tenor announced, rising with an air of helpful eagerness. "When they get riled, they skin a feller alive real slow."

"Now, *that's* something I've never tried," the Kid declared, although he did not mention that he had once seen the gory results of such a torture having been inflicted.[1] "You wouldn't want to come show me how it's done?"

"Why, sure," the stocky Texan agreed. "Only, I don't want nobody else 'round to watch. The Kiowas who taught me wouldn't want other folks learning how it's done. And, seeing's how it's me's who's doing the showing, I claim the big 'n' to work on."

"You must have some Kiowa blood yourself," the Kid

said in a complaining tone. "I've allus heard they don't have much hospitality."

Although Cunningham had lost most of the color from his cheeks and was about to speak, he was not permitted to do so. Before he could utter a word or do anything to save himself, the bowie knife had been returned to its sheath and he was being hustled from the room. Given a warning by the Kid that nobody must follow no matter what they heard, the pair dragged their limply struggling captive outside and left the door open. After a few minutes had elapsed in a silence that could almost be felt, a series of bloodcurdling screams arose from the darkness. Even Madsen looked startled by what he heard, and the rest of the occupants showed a variety of emotions. However, none of them offered to leave.

"He was some tougher than I figured," the Kid remarked, strolling into the room wiping the blade of his knife on what Wilbran, for one, recognized as being the shirt Cunningham had been wearing. "I had to lend that gent a hand. Anyways, I reckon we'll know when to stop now. Come on, *hombre*, let's give her a whirl with *you*."

"No!" the young outlaw screeched, and threw himself to his knees at Madsen's feet. "Don't let 'em do it, Marshal. Miss Hardin's not been hurt, nor will be, and I'll tell you where they've got her."

"What the hell happened out there, Kid?" the peace officer demanded, after Wilbran had given the required information and offered to guide him to the place where Betty was being held. "And where's S—*Eph Tenor*?"

"*Happened?*" the black-dressed Texan inquired, looking as innocent as a church full of choirboys waiting to meet the bishop. "Why, good ole Eph's looking after that jasper, he plumb swooned a swoon when he saw all the blood."

"What blood?" Madsen demanded.

"That come when I busted him on the nose," the Kid replied. "Where did you reckon it'd come from?"[2]

---

1. *Told in* A TOWN CALLED YELLOWDOG.

2. *We realize the locale given in this chapter differs from the description of how the two young outlaws were arrested in the incident from which the narrative is an "expansion," but we are assured by our informants the version herein is what really took place.*

CHAPTER SEVENTEEN

I'LL *KILL* HER

"He'sh the fastesh gun in
   Texshush,
He'sh the bravesh of 'em all,
In a shreet you'd walk right by him,
'Caush he don't sthand very tall,
Comesh trouble he'sh the bravest,
Fights like a Comanche dog,
He'sh from the Rio Hondo country,
And hish name ish Dushty Fog."

Listening to what would have been a pleasant tenor
voice if it had not had a timbre suggesting the vocal cords
were loosened more than somewhat by Old Stump Blaster
or some other potent liquor, Betty Hardin could hardly
restrain a smile. She had heard the song rendered properly
far too many times not to be aware that it was coming
from the lips of the Ysabel Kid. What was more, she was
just as aware that he never took more than an occasional
beer, so deduced it was intended to warn her that help was
on its way.

"The question is," the beautiful little black-haired girl

mused, watching by the light of the small lantern that was the only illumination showing how the four men around the room were reacting, "how does that crazy, baby-faced part Comanche intend to supply it?"

At no time during the ride to the ranch, especially after Jack Cunningham—who she sensed would be the most dangerous of them and clearly still bore her a grudge for the way she had responded to his actions during the holdup—had departed with Simcock Wilbran, had Betty felt herself in any way threatened by or in danger from the rest of the gang. Rather, they had shown great consideration for her well-being and one or another had repeatedly inquired whether she would care to take a rest. By the time they had brought her to what was obviously their hideout, for the first time in her life she was thankful for the blood-and-thunder books upon which they had based their notions of how outlaws should behave.

Betty was no middle class–middle management snob, taught from early childhood by their parents that every form of entertainment popular with the masses—and such Western-based literature in particular—was invariably of inferior quality and therefore below their great intellect. Rather, she enjoyed reading the imaginative offerings of men like Ned Buntline and never forgot how long it took her cousin, Dusty Fog, to live down having been described in the *Police Gazette* as "a dashingly handsome figure in long-fringed buckskins, with streaming curly golden hair and a magnificently flowing moustache." She felt she would enjoy them even more from now on.

Studying the small and dilapidated log cabin, which had some rude furnishings, Betty had concluded that it was obviously deserted instead of having been taken over with its occupants murdered. Once inside, she had started to play upon the quartet's attempts to prove they were the kind of outlaws they had believed Jesse James to be as the result of their readings. What was more, as any member of the OD Connected crew would have been all too willing to declare in her absence, she was the girl to get things done the way she wanted them.

Starting by refusing to enter such a hovel, as she pretended to believe Jesse James would never expect a *lady* prisoner being held for ransom to stay in such dirty condition, she had had her captors clean it before condescending to go in. They had also used the tarps from their bedrolls to keep out the rain that started and, she realized, was likely to wash away all traces of their tracks. Then, on finding how primitive was the way Thomas Bower began to prepare for cooking, she had taken over the task. However, before commencing to make them a better meal than they had had for many days—it being something she had been well taught by Dusty's mother and other distaff members of the Hardin, Fog, and Blaze clan—she had *insisted* that they all go to wash and make themselves presentable to her demanding satisfaction before allowing them to eat.

Despite there having been numerous opportunities for Betty to escape, she had not attempted to do so. She had realized that, while allowing her to take considerable liberties in such small matters, their attitude could easily change should they feel their chances of obtaining the sizable ransom they anticipated were being put in jeopardy. With the passing of time, Jesse Wilbran had grown annoyed rather than concerned over the continued absence of his brother and Cunningham. He had blamed the latter for this and threatened to take severe measures when they finally got around to returning. Betty had wondered whether the ensuing friction would offer the chance she was willing to take to either escape or turn the tables even more completely on her captors.

Such an eventuality would, the black-haired little girl had thought with a mischievous delight, give her consid-

erable moral and actual advantage over Dusty, Mark
Counter, the Kid, and Waco if she succeeded in doing this
without needing their assistance. There were times when
they failed to show the deference accorded by the other
members of the crew, and she liked nothing better than to
gain a brief period of ascendancy. There was nothing ma-
licious in her feelings. Rather, these arose from the free
and easy relationship she had with all of them, and she
would never have thought to cause any embarrassment for
them by her actions.

"What the hell?" Jesse Wilbran growled. "Who's *that*?"

The words were a purely rhetorical question.

What was more, an answer of sorts was soon forthcoming.

"Hello the housh'!" the same drunken-sounding voice
yelled as the approaching hoofbeats came to a stop a short
distance from the building. "The namesh Waco from Taik-
shush 'n' the boysh've feshed me 'long to ride owlhoot
withsh you-all."

"There's only one of 'em," Frank Dobson reported from
the window to which he had hurried and drawn back the
flour sack that served as an extemporized curtain. "Only,
he's got Sim 'n' Jack hanging across their saddles like
they're plumb tuckered out 'n' sleeping."

"Liquored out, more like," Graham Taylor guessed in an
envious fashion, having been an unwillingly acquiescent
recipient of some of Betty's treatment.

"There's something don't seem *right* about this!" Wilbran growled, and pulled a jackknife from his trousers
pocket to open its main blade.

"What's up, Jess?" Bower inquired.

"I'm not surprised as how they'd fetch along somebody
else, happen they got liquored up someplace 'n' 'llowed as
how he wanted to join up with us," Wilbran answered, and
moved swiftly to Betty's side before she realized what was

intended. Grasping her by the right shoulder with his left hand, he drew her to her feet and, keeping her in front of him by passing his other arm across the front of her upper torso, held the blade of the knife against her neck. "Keep quiet and don't make no fuss, ma'am. I'll 'pologize should I be wrong. Only, I don't reckon as how Sim in particular'd forget to let him know about our secret signal's has to be give'. Go out there 'n' see what's doing, Frank, Tom."

"Sure, Jess," Dobson assented.

HAVING extracted the information that was required, the Ysabel Kid and U.S. Deputy Marshal Chris Madsen had quickly decided upon a plan of campaign.

The strategy was based upon the conclusions both had reached with regard to the quality of the men they were going up against, plus what they had been told by Flint Major—whose judgment they respected—about the way the holdup was carried out.

"They're playing at being gentlemen road agents like they reckon Dingus James to be," the shotgun guard had assessed. "That showed in everything they did. Which being, Miss Hardin'll be safe and treated right—just so long as nothing happens to spook them. Once that happens, they'll be dangerous as stick-teased rattlers 'n' twice as unpredictable."

Arranging for Cunningham to be held for him by Big Win, who he knew would do as he required, the peace officer had asked Eph Tenor to continue being of assistance. The offer was accepted as willingly as the others had been, even without the stocky Texan waiting to find out what would be required of him. When told, he had not changed his mind or done more than hint that he considered a comfortable pillow of suitable dimensions would make the part he played considerably easier. Without inquiring why it was needed, as she had not heard what was intended, the massive woman had sought to give a further example of her willingness to help the law by producing one that met with Tenor's requirements.

Guided by Sim Wilbran, who lacked the courage to do otherwise despite certain misgivings he was feeling, the trio had been brought across the range. On being told they world very soon be coming into sight of the house, there had been a pause while he was gagged and had his legs fastened together by a pigging thong the Kid had produced. His wrists already being secured by the peace officer's handcuffs, he was draped belly down over the saddle of his horse. Declaring that doing so would plumb ruin him socially, happen it was heard about in Denton County, Texas, Tenor had adopted a similar posture with his fine-looking bay gelding, the mare to which he had referred having been left at Bent's Ford. With that done, although Madsen stopped as soon as the house came into view, the advance was resumed to the accompaniment of the Kid's "drunken" singing.

At first, everything seemed to be going as planned.

Then, however, Sim decided to do something to make amends for having helped cause the predicament for his brother and the rest of the gang.

The thought had been with the young outlaw ever since he had discovered that, far from having been tortured to death, Jack Cunningham was suffering from nothing worse than being stripped to the waist and having a bloody nose. He had intended to warn his remaining companions in some fashion before they could be captured and rely upon Jesse, for whose intelligence he had a very high regard, to save him. The way he had been treated made doing so more difficult, but he thought he had a way out.

"Looks like Sim 'n' Jack's been having them a good time, Jess," Dobson called as he and Bower emerged from the building each carrying a revolver. "That's hell of a fine hoss

the Texan's afork. Likely Jess'll take it for his own afore he
lets him join up with us."

"We'd best get 'em off 'n' inside," Bower supplemented,
sounding equally envious but failing to notice that "Cunningham" was hanging over the saddle of a much finer
animal than previously. Tucking the revolver into his waistband, he walked forward, with the other outlaw duplicating
his actions. A thought struck him as he realized that only
"Belle Starr" had received a share of the loot, and he went
on without drawing any particular conclusions on the matter. "Where the hell did they get the money from?"

If Libby Craddock had been alive to hear the question,
she would have discovered that she was given less than the
sum of money sent to her by Jesse.

With Dobson walking by toward where Tenor was hanging limply, Bower began to get an impression that
something was not quite as it should be. Belatedly, he realized that Sim was behaving in a fashion different from
"Cunningham" by grunting loudly and writhing around.
Next he caught a glimpse of something metallic glistening
on the waving wrists of the younger brother and he was
filled with a sensation of alarm.

"Look out, Jess'!" Bower screeched rather than just
yelled, and he grabbed for the butt of the revolver.

Before the draw could be brought anywhere near com-
pletion, the young outlaw might have considered himself
fortunate that he was treated in such a comparatively
harmless fashion. Coming from its stirrup iron, the Kid's
right foot rose to kick him under the chin. The attack came
unexpectedly and with a force that caused him to topple
backwards. Almost as soon as he alighted, his assailant was
plunging down to kneel astride his torso. Topped by the
most savage face he had ever encountered, he saw an enormous knife pass before his amazed gaze to rest its razor-
sharp blade against his neck, which was already sore from

having been compelled by Betty Hardin to be subjected to a much closer shave than it usually received. Nor, although he did not notice at that moment, was Dobson being treated in too different a fashion.

"*Surprise!*" Tenor drawled quietly, and delivered a blow from the barrel of the Colt Peacemaker he had held unseen to the top of the bare head presented so admirably for such treatment. The other outlaw went down to be treated in the same fashion as the first, except that the gun's muzzle was used to enforce a desire for silence. Then, knowing his companion, he went on with some urgency, "We don't need us no bloody *nose* this time, Lon!"

Unfortunately for the rescuers, they had not moved quite quickly enough.

"You out there!" yelled a voice filled with more alarm than menace from inside the building. "I've got Miss Hardin with a knife to her throat. I'll *kill* her 'less'n you turn my men loose and ride the hell away from here!"

STANDING rock steady, Betty Hardin listened to the warning given by the leader of her captors. She realized that the moment of danger was rapidly approaching. There was a note of something close to panic in Jesse Wilbran's voice, and she knew that, regardless of his pose as the noble and gallant outlaw, he was quite capable of carrying out the threat should he feel driven to do so.

"Don't be *loco, hombre!*" the Ysabel Kid's voice came back. "Give it up. We've got the place surrounded and you can't get anywhere near the hosses you've got out here, much less getting the hobbles off 'em."

"I've got *her!*" Jesse repeated, while Betty was wondering whether the black-dressed Texan had seen or was just guessing at the way in which she had insisted the horses were given attention before their users carried out her instructions for them to wash and shave before allowing them to eat. Looking out through the open door, she discovered with relief that she could see what was happening outside and was sure the same applied to her rescuers where the part of the room's interior that mattered was concerned. Failing to duplicate her observations, her captor was going on, "So either you do what I say, else—!"

At which everything began to go wrong for the outlaw leader.

Giving what sounded like a heartrending groan, Betty started to slump a trifle in her captor's grasp. Feeling this, he was unable to prevent himself from relaxing both hold and position of the jackknife's blade. A moment later, the top of his right boot was subjected to a painful stamp. Then his left arm was grasped by two surprisingly strong little hands. Then the black-haired girl began to bend her knees as she had been taught by the man who had given her instruction in how to do such things.[1] The leverage she was able to apply caused him to turn a half-somersault over her shoulder and alight with a resounding thud on the floor with all the breath being driven from his lungs.

Although Betty had set herself free, she realized that the danger to herself was not yet at an end.

"Stand still!" the remaining outlaw yelled, pointing his revolver at Betty as she straightened up and started to turn his way.

"Come on, now, Ham," the girl said quietly yet calmly, making no attempt to reach for the Remington Double Derringer that she was carrying in its concealed holster under the left side of her bolero jacket without its presence having been even suspected. "You aren't going to shoot me, so drop the gun before something really bad happens to you."

Letting out something close to a sob, Taylor did as he was told.

"Why hello, Lon," Betty said in tones of well-simulated

surprise as the Kid burst into the cabin with his left hand holding the bowie knife and his right grasping the butt of the Dragoon Colt. "Fancy meeting you here."

"Did any of 'em—!" the Kid demanded savagely, although he could see that the contingency to which he was referring had not taken place.

"Good Lord, *no*," Betty replied. "They've all treated me like perfect gentlemen from the beginning. I've never even once had to take my little old John D out." Rapidly approaching hooves drummed and, a few seconds later, the other two rescuers came into the room. "Why, heavens to Betsy, it's you, S—!"

"Shucks!" the Kid exclaimed. "I'd clean forgot as how you knowed *Eph Tenor* from up Denton way."

"Oh, I do," the girl replied, and something in the way she spoke caused the Indian-dark Texan to look hard at her. "I most certainly *do*. Would you take me outside, please, Marshal? I feel a little faint."

"I tell you, gents," Taylor said, watching the peace officer and Betty leave. "I'm not sorry to see her go. That is one *mean*-natured li'l gal. On top of all the a-cleaning and a-dusting out she made us give this place, would you believe she not only made me shave so close I thought I'd peel my hide, but she made me go out 'n' wash my hands agin 'cause she allowed I didn't get 'em clean enough first time."

"Yep, that's our boss lady," the Kid declared in genuine sympathy, glancing around the unexpectedly neat and tidy room and deducing how this had been brought about and wondering if there was any condition in the whole wide world that could make her even a little faint. "She's sure enough *mean*!"

"By the way, Marshal," Betty was saying at that moment, as she looked to where Dobson and Bower were sitting on the ground looking scared. "What are you going to do with them?"

"Take 'em afore Judge Parker at Fort Smith for trial," U.S. Deputy Marshal Chris Madsen replied.[2]

"Is that necessary?" the girl inquired.

"They've bust the law even worse'n holding up the coach to Bent's Ford when they took you to hold for ransom," the peace officer pointed out.

"I know," Betty admitted. "But is it necessary to take them before *him*? Couldn't it be handled at local level?"

"Well, I—!"

"They never harmed me, or were even in any way disrespectful. And I'm willing to bet that, after the fright they've just been handed, they'll never try anything like it again."

"It's the way—!" Madsen began.

"I wonder how folks would feel if they knew you'd been riding all day long without knowing you had Sam Bass as a member of your posse?" Betty queried. Looking as if butter would be hard put to melt in her mouth, she went on, "These bunch don't know him, and I know Lon won't tell. Nor would I, not deliberately, but I do declare I'm such a li'l ole blabbermouth I might let it slip out, by *accident*, of course."

"All right, Miss Hardin," Madsen said with a grin, envisioning the amusement that would arise if it should be heard by the other two "Guardsmen"—who he guessed would be the only persons to be told—how he had had the well-known Texas outlaw accompany him and the Kid. As had many another man when trying to oppose the will of the beautiful and very competent granddaughter of Ole Devil Hardin, he concluded he might as well surrender with good grace. "You win. I'll let Duke Bent hand them their not-deserved needings as justice of the peace down this way. Then I'm going to tell Mr. Eph Tenor that we'd sooner he didn't stick around racing that Denton mare he's allus boasting about."

"AND now, Mr. Loncey Dalton Ysabel," Betty Hardin said as she and the black-dressed Texan were standing in the room she was given on being returned to Bent's Ford a short while earlier. "What's the game?"

"Huh?" the Kid inquired, genuinely puzzled.

"Why do you keep acting so all-fired eager to please me?" Betty explained, looking distinctly suspicious.

"It's all on account of my loving 'n' respect—!"

The words were brought to an abrupt end by something that only three men in the world could have done without very quickly having regretted the decision to do so.

"I want the *truth*, like you reckon your Comanche side always tells," Betty declared, grasping the Indian-dark Texan's left ear to give it a twist. "So start to spitting it out, pronto!"

"Easy there, boss lady!" the Kid protested. "It's fastened onto the side and not meant to be turned upside—!"

"The *truth*!" Betty demanded.

"Calf rope!" the Kid yelled. "I should've knowed there was something bad coming when Waco was so all-fired eager to take them stud hosses to Mark's uncle's spread up north of Mulrooney. Sneaky young cuss!"

"And was there?"

"There sure as sin's for sale in Cowtown was. A young feller as had helped us out more'n somewhat when we was running the law got hisself set for marrying to the next-richest family in town, Freddie 'n' Dusty being the first."

"Go on!" Betty commanded, releasing the ear. "Get to the white meat!"

"Well, we floating outfit boys was all invited to the wedding," the Kid obliged, looking distressed and shamefaced. "And real *fancy* 'n' high-toned it was going to be. We was

told by Freddie—who I allus took for being as good a
friend of mine as *you* are—!"

"Keep going!" the girl ordered. "Trying to butter me up
won't work."

"Well, she said's how we was going to have to dress up,"
the Kid obliged, and gave a shudder at the recollection of
what was to follow. "It'd mean wearing a frock coat, shirt
with a collar and cravat or some such, 'n' even worse, a
high silk hat."

"So you ran out on Dusty and Mark?" Betty guessed.

"Wasn't that ways at all," the Kid protested with what
he hoped would sound like indignation but was more indicative to the girl of his having a guilty conscience over
his behavior by deserting his *amigos* in such a craven fashion. "Hell, Dusty's used to wearing such fancy doodads and
I allus reckon Mark even *likes* doing it. Which I'd still've
stood by 'em like a man, 'cepting I remembered as how
you'd said you'd be waiting down here to Bent's to get us
safe back to home 'n' concluded I'd best put aside my
pleasuring to come 'n' do it."

"I'll accept that, although thousands *wouldn't*," Betty
said with no sign of the merriment bubbling inside her.
"But I wouldn't want to be in your shoes when Dusty and
Mark get here after what you did to them."[3]

---

1. *The identity of the man who gave Betty Hardin instruction
in various methods of unarmed self-defense is given in various volumes of the* Civil War *and* Floating Outfit *series.*

2. *Having been appointed to the Federal Court for the Western
District of Oklahoma, the sentences inflicted by Isaac C. Parker
were frequently of such severity that he had become known as the
"Hanging Judge."*

3. *When asked by the Ysabel Kid why he had saved the life of a lawman who might be considering arresting him, Sam Bass said his only motivation was there might not be another tenor available to help them sing in a quartet when they got back to Bent's Ford.*

APPENDIX ONE

Wanting a son and learning that his wife, Electra, could not have any more children, Vincent Charles Boyd gave his only daughter, Belle,[1] a thorough training in several subjects not normally regarded as being necessary for the upbringing of a wealthy Southron girl. At seventeen, she could ride—astride or sidesaddle—as well as any of her male neighbors, men who were to help provide the Confederate States with its superlative cavalry. In addition, she was a skilled performer with an *épée de combat* or a saber,[2] an excellent shot with any kind of handheld firearm, and an expert at *savate*, the French style of foot and fist boxing. All these accomplishments were to be very useful to her as time went by.

Shortly before the commencement of the War Between the States, a mob of pro-Union supporters, led by two "liberal" agitators who fled north immediately after, stormed the Boyd plantation. Before they were driven off by the girl and the family's Negro servants, they had murdered her parents and burned her home to the ground. On recovering from the wound she sustained in the fighting, hostilities having broken out between the South and the North, she joined the successful spy ring organized by her cousin,

Rose Greenhow.[3] Wanting to find and take revenge upon the leaders of the mob, Belle was not content to operate in one locality. Instead, she undertook the dangerous task of delivering other agents' information to the appropriate Confederate authorities. Adding an ability at disguise and in producing different dialects to her other accomplishments, she graduated to handling even more important and risky assignments, attaining such proficiency that she won the sobriquet "Rebel Spy." On two missions, she worked with Captain Dustine Edward Marsden "Dusty" Fog, Company "C," Texas Light Cavalry.[4] Another had first brought her into contact with the Ysabel Kid,[5] and later, accompanied by him and his father, Sam Ysabel, she had concluded her quest of vengeance upon the men responsible for the murder of her parents.[6]

While the "Yankees" were given reason to hate the Rebel Spy when she was engaged in her duties against them during the War, the majority had no cause to feel other than gratitude after peace was brought about by the meeting at the Appomattox Court House. On signing the oath of allegiance to the Union, she was enrolled in the United States Secret Service. Despite all the trouble she had given that organization throughout the hostilities, she served it loyally and with equal efficiency. Her participation in thwarting a plot to assassinate President Ulysses Simpson Grant prevented friction and possibly another war between the Southern and Northern states.[7] Assisted by Martha "Calamity Jane" Canary[8] and Belle Starr,[9] she brought to an end the reign of terror caused by a murderous gang of female outlaws.[10] With the aid of Dusty Fog and other members of the OD Connected ranch's floating outfit, she broke up the Brotherhood for Southern Freedom.[11] In the same company, she prevented diplomatic difficulties between the United States and Haiti.[12] She joined forces once more with Belle Starr and the Ysabel Kid when involved in the efforts of the international master criminal Octavius Xavier "The Ox" Guille-mot, to gain possession of James Bowie's knife.[13] Assisted by Calamity Jane and Captain Patrick Reeder of the British Secret Service, she wrecked two attempts by European anarchists to create hostility between the United States and Great—as it was then—Britain.[14] Assisted by the successful British lady criminal, Amelia Penelope Diana "Benkers" Benkinsop, she dealt with the man who had sold arms to the plotters.[15]

---

1. *According to the world's foremost fiction genealogist, Philip Jose Farmer, author of, among numerous other works,* TARZAN ALIVE, The Definitive Biography of Lord Greystoke *and* DOC SAVAGE, His Apocalyptic Life—*with whom we have consulted, Belle Boyd was the maternal grand-aunt of Jane, Lady Greystoke, née Porter, whose biography is recorded in the* TARZAN OF THE APES *series of biographies by Edgar Rice Burroughs.*

2. *An épée de combat is used mainly for thrusting, and the saber was originally intended chiefly for slashing from the back of a horse.*

3. *One incident in Rose Greenhow's career is recorded in* KILL DUSTY FOG!

4. *Told in:* THE COLT AND THE SABRE *and* THE REBEL SPY.

5. *Told in:* THE BLOODY BORDER.

5a. *Details of Captain Dustine Edward Marsden "Dusty" Fog's and the Ysabel Kid's careers are given in the* Civil War *and* Floating Outfit *series.*

6. *Told in* RENEGADE.

7. *Told in* THE HOODED RIDERS.

8. *Information regarding the career of Martha "Calamity Jane" Canary is to be found in the* Calamity Jane *series, and she makes "guest" appearances in* Part One, "The Bounty on Belle Starr's Scalp," TROUBLED RANGE; *its "expansion,"* CALAMITY, MARK AND BELLE; Part One, "Better Than Calamity," THE WILDCATS; THE BAD BUNCH; THE FORTUNE HUNTERS; Part Six, "Mrs. Wild Bill," J.T.'S LADIES; Part Four, "Draw Poker's Such A *Simple* Game," J.T.'S LADIES RIDE AGAIN *("costarring with the lady outlaw, Belle Starr, q.v.)*; Part Seven, "Deadwood, August the 2nd, 1876," J.T.'S HUNDRETH; Part Four, "A Wife For Dusty Fog," THE SMALL TEXAN *and* GUNS IN THE NIGHT.

9. *Belle Starr makes "guest" appearances in* RANGELAND HERCULES; THE BAD BUNCH; CARDS AND COLTS; THE CODE OF DUSTY FOG; THE GENTLE GIANT; HELL IN THE PALO DURO; GO BACK TO HELL; Part Four, "A Lady Known as Belle," THE HARD RIDERS; Part Two, "We Hang Horse Thieves High," J.T.'S HUNDREDTH *and* Part Six, "Mrs. Wild Bill," J.T.'S LADIES. *The circumstances of her death are told in* GUNS IN THE NIGHT.

9a. *The lady outlaw "stars," no pun intended, in* WANTED! BELLE STARR.

9b. We are frequently asked why it is that the "Belle Starr" we describe is so different from a photograph that appears in various books. The researches of Philip Jose Farmer, q.v., *have established that the lady for whom we are biographer is not the same person as another equally famous bearer of the name. However, the present-day members of the Counter family who supplied us with information respecting her have asked Mr. Farmer and us to keep her true identity a secret, and this we intend to do.*

10. *Told in* THE BAD BUNCH.

11. *Told in* TO ARMS! TO ARMS! IN DIXIE *and* THE SOUTH WILL RISE AGAIN.

11a. *"Floating outfit": a group of four to six cowhands employed by a large ranch to work the more distant sections of the property. Taking food in a chuck wagon, or a "greasy sack" on the back of a mule, they would be away from the ranch house for long periods and so were selected for their honesty, loyalty, reliability, and capability in all aspects of their work. Because the owner of the OD Connected ranch, General Jackson Baines "Ole Devil" Hardin, was prominent in the affairs of Texas, members of its floating outfit were frequently sent to assist such of his friends who found themselves in difficulties or endangered.*

11b. Details of the career of General Jackson Baines "Ole Devil" Hardin are given in the Ole Devil Hardin, Civil War *and* Floating Outfit *series, and in* Part Four, "Mr. Colt's Revolving Cylinder Pistol," J.T.'S HUNDREDTH. *His death is reported in* DOC LEROY, M.D.

12. *Told in* SET A-FOOT.

13. *Told in* THE QUEST FOR BOWIE'S BLADE.

14. *Told in* THE REMITTANCE KID *and* THE WHIP AND THE WAR LANCE.

14a. *The researches of Philip Jose Farmer, q.v., have established that Captain Patrick Reeder (later Major General Sir, K.C.B, V.C., D.S.O., M.C., and Bar) was the uncle of the celebrated British detective Mr. Jeremiah Golden Reeder, whose biography appears in* ROOM 13, THE MIND OF MR. J.G. REEDER, RED ACES, MR. J.G. REEDER RETURNS, THE GUV'NOR, *and* TERROR KEEP, *by Edgar Wallace.*

14b. *Mr. Jeremiah Golden Reeder's organization plays a prominent part in the events we recorded as* "CAP" FOG, TEXAS RANGER, MEET MR. J.G. REEDER; THE RETURN OF RAPIDO CLINT AND MR. J.G. REEDER *and* RAPIDO CLINT STRIKES BACK.

15. *Told in* Part Five, "The Butcher's Fiery End," J.T.'S LADIES.

15a. *Some other activities of the very competent British lady criminal Amelia Penelope Diana "Benkers" Benkinsop, during her visit to the United States in the mid-1870s, are recorded in* BE-GUINAGE IS DEAD! *and Part Three, "Birds of a Feather,"* WANTED! BELLE STARR.

15b. *The daughter of the "Benkers" referred to in* Footnote 15a *makes a "guest" appearance in* Case Two, "The Feminine Touch for Company 'Z,'" MORE JUSTICE FROM COMPANY "Z."

15c. *Information about the daughter of the above "Benkers"—who also followed the family tradition of retaining the full name regardless of who the father might be—Miss Amelia Penelope Diana Benkinsop, G.C., M.A., B.Sc. (Oxon.), owner of Benkinsop's Academy for the Daughters of Gentlefolk in England, is given in* BLONDE GENIUS; Part One, "Fifteen the Hard Way," J.T.'S LADIES *and Part Two, "A Case of Blackmail,"* J.T.'S LADIES RIDE AGAIN.

15d. *BLONDE GENIUS is the rarest of our books. To date, copies that have passed through the hands of the now regrettably defunct J.T. Edson Appreciation Society and have been auctioned by us for charity have realized from avid collectors: £60.00; U.S. $65.00; £35.00; U.S. $30.00, and three at £25.00 each.*

APPENDIX TWO

Raven Head, only daughter of Chief Long Walker, war leader of the *Pehnane*—Wasp, Quick Stinger, Raider—Comanche's Dog Soldier lodge and his French Creole *pairaivo*,[1] married a Irish-Kentuckian adventurer, Big Sam Ysabel, but died giving birth to their first child.

Baptized "Loncey Dalton Ysabel," the boy was raised after the fashion of the *Nemenuh*.[2] With his father away from the camp for much of the time, engaged upon the family's combined businesses of mustanging—catching and breaking wild horses[3]—and smuggling, his education had largely been left in the hands of his maternal grandfather.[4] From Long Walker, he learned all those things a Comanche warrior must know: how to ride the wildest freshly caught mustang, or make a trained animal subservient to his will while "raiding"—a polite name for the favorite pastime of the male *Nemenuh*, stealing horses—to follow the faintest tracks and just as effectively conceal signs of his own passing[5]; to locate hidden enemies, or keep out of sight himself when the need arose; to move in silence on the darkest of nights, or through the thickest cover; to know the ways of wild creatures[6] and, in some cases, imitate their calls so well that others of their kind were fooled.[7]

The boy proved a most excellent pupil at all the subjects. Nor were practical means of protecting himself forgotten. Not only did he learn to use all the traditional weapons of the Comanche[8]; when he had come into the possession of firearms, he had inherited his father's Kentuckian skill at shooting with a rifle and, while not *real* fast on the draw—taking slightly over a second to bring up his Colt Second Model of 1848 Dragoon revolver and fire, whereas a tophand could do it in practically half that time—he could perform passably with it. Furthermore, he won his *Nemenuh* "man-name," *Cuchilo,* Spanish for "Knife," by his exceptional ability at wielding one. In fact, it was claimed by those best qualified to judge that he could equal the alleged designer in performing with the massive and special type of blade that bore the name of Colonel James Bowie.[9]

Joining his father in smuggling expeditions along the Rio Grande, the boy became known to the Mexicans of the border country as *Cabrito*—the Spanish name for a young goat—a nickname that arose out of hearing white men refer to him as the "Ysabel Kid," but it was spoken *very* respectfully in that context. Smuggling was not an occupation to attract the meek and mild of manner, yet even the roughest and toughest of the bloody border's denizens came to acknowledge that it did not pay to rile up Big Sam Ysabel's son. The education received by the Kid had not been calculated to develop any overinflated belief in the sanctity of human life. When crossed, he dealt with the situation like a *Pehnane* Dog Soldier—to which war lodge of savage and *most* efficient warriors he had earned initiation—swiftly and in an effectively deadly manner.

During the War Between the States, the Kid and his father had commenced by riding as scouts for Colonel John Singleton "the Gray Ghost" Mosby. Soon, however, their specialized knowledge and talents were diverted to having them collect and deliver to the Confederate States' authorities in Texas supplies that had been purchased in Mexico, or run through the blockade by the United States Navy into Matamoros. It was hard and dangerous work,[10] but never more so than the two occasions when they became engaged in assignments with Belle "the Rebel Spy" Boyd.[11]

Soon after the war ended, Sam Ysabel was murdered. While hunting down the killers, the Kid met Captain Dustine Edward Marsden "Dusty" Fog and Mark Counter. When the mission in which they were engaged was brought to its successful conclusion, learning the Kid no longer wished to go on either smuggling or mustanging, the small Texan offered him employment at the OD Connected ranch. It had been in the capacity as scout rather than ordinary cowhand that he was required and his talents in that field were frequently of the greatest use as a member of the floating outfit.[12]

The acceptance of the job by the Kid was of the greatest benefit all around. Dusty acquired another loyal friend who was ready to stick to him through any kind of peril. The ranch obtained the services of an extremely capable and efficient fighting man. For his part, the Kid was turned from a life of petty crime—with the ever-present danger of having his illicit activities develop into serious law breaking—and became a useful and law-abiding member of society. Peace officers and honest citizens might have found cause to feel grateful for that. His *Nemenuh* upbringing would have made him a terrible and murderous outlaw if he had been driven into a life of violent crime.

Obtaining his first repeating rifle—a Winchester Model of 1866, although at first known as the "New Improved Henry," nicknamed the "Old Yellowboy" because of its brass frame—while in Mexico with Dusty and Mark, the Kid had soon become an expert in its use. At the First

Cochise County Fair in Arizona, despite circumstances compelling him to use a weapon with which he was not familiar,[13] he won the first prize in the rifle-shooting competition against stiff opposition. The prize was one of the legendary Winchester Model of 1873 rifles that qualified for the honored designation "One of a Thousand."[14]

It was, in part, through the efforts of the Kid that the majority of the Comanche bands agreed to go on the reservation, following attempts to ruin the signing of the treaty.[15] It was to a large extent due to his efforts that the outlaw town of Hell was located and destroyed.[16] Aided by Annie "Is-A-Man" Singing Bear—a girl of mixed parentage who gained the distinction of becoming accepted as a *Nemenuh* warrior[17]—he played a major part in preventing the attempted theft of Morton Lewis's ranch, provoking trouble with the *Kweharehnuh* Comanche.[18] To help a young man out of difficulties caused by a gang of card cheats, he teamed up with the lady outlaw, Belle Starr.[19] When he accompanied Martha "Calamity Jane" Canary to inspect a ranch she had inherited, they became involved in as dangerous a situation as either had ever faced.[20]

Remaining at the OD Connected ranch until he, Dusty, and Mark met their deaths while on a hunting trip to Kenya shortly after the turn of the century, his descendants continued to be associated with the Hardin, Fog, and Blaze clan and the Counter family.[21]

---

1. Pairaivo: *first, or favorite, wife. As is the case with the other Comanche terms, this is a phonetic spelling.*

2. Nemenuh: *"the People," the Comanches' name for themselves and their nation. Members of other tribes with whom they came into contact called them, frequently with good cause, the* "Tshaoh," *the* "Enemy People."

3. *A description of the way in which mustangers operated is given in* .44 CALBIRE MAN *and* A HORSE CALLED MO-GOLLON.

4. *Told in* COMANCHE.

5. *An example of how the Ysabel Kid could conceal his tracks is given in Part One, "The Half Breed,"* THE HALF BREED.

6. *Two examples of how the Ysabel Kid's knowledge of wild animals was turned to good use are given in* OLD MOCCASINS ON THE TRAIL *and* BUFFALO ARE COMING!

7. *An example of how well the Ysabel Kid could impersonate the call of a wild animal is recorded in Part Three, "A Wolf's a Knowing Critter,"* J.T.'S HUNDREDTH.

8. *One occasion when the Ysabel Kid employed his skill with traditional Comanche weapons is described in* RIO GUNS.

9. *Some researchers claim that the actual designer of the knife that became permanently attached to Colonel James Bowie's name was his oldest brother, Rezin Pleasant. Although it is generally conceded that the maker was James Black, a master cutler in Arkanas, some authorities state that it was manufactured by Jesse Cliffe, a white blacksmith employed by the Bowie family on their plantation in Rapides Parish, Louisiana.*

9a. *What happened to James Bowie's knife after his death in the final assault of the siege of the Alamo Mission, San Antonio de Bexar, Texas, on March 6, 1836, is told in* TEXAS FURY *and* THE QUEST FOR BOWIE'S BLADE.

9b. *Since all of James Black's knives were custom made, there were variations in their dimensions. The specimen owned by the Ysabel Kid had a blade eleven and a half inches in length, two and a half inches wide, and a quarter of an inch thick at the guard. According to William "Bo" Randall, of Randall-Made Knives, Orlando, Florida—a master cutler and authority upon the subject in his own right—James Bowie's knife weighed forty-three ounces, having a blade eleven inches long, two and a quarter inches wide, and three-eighths of an inch thick. His company's Model 12 "Smithsonian" bowie knife—one of which is owned by James Allenvale "Bunduki" Gunn, details of whose career can be found in the Bunduki series—is modeled on it.*

9c. *One thing all bowie knives have in common, regardless of dimensions, is a "clip point." The otherwise unsharpened "back" of the blade joins and becomes an extension of the main cutting surface in a concave arc, whereas a "spear point"—which is less utilitarian—is formed by the two sides coming together in symmetrical curves.*

10. *An occasion when Big Sam Ysabel went on a mission without his son is recorded in* THE DEVIL GUN.

11. *Told in* THE BLOODY BORDER *and* BACK TO THE BLOODY BORDER.

12. *"Floating outfit": a group of four to six cowhands employed by a large ranch to work the more distant sections of the property. Taking food in a chuck wagon, or a "greasy sack" on the back of a pack mule, they would be away from the ranch house for long periods and so were selected for their honesty, reliability, loyalty, and capability in all aspects of their work. Because of the prominence of General Jackson Baines "Ole Devil" Hardin in the affairs of Texas, the OD Connected's floating outfit was frequently sent to assist such of his friends who found themselves in difficulties or endangered.*

13. *The circumstances are described in* GUN WIZARD.

14. *When manufacturing the extremely popular Winchester Model of 1873 rifle—which they claimed to be the "Gun Which Won the West"—the makers selected all those barrels found to shoot with exceptional accuracy to be fitted with set triggers and given a special fine finish. Originally, these were inscribed "1 of 1,000," but this was later changed to script: "One of a Thousand." However, the title was a considerable understatement. Only one hundred and*

thirty-six out of a total production of 720,610 qualified for the distinction. Those of a grade lower were to be designated "One of a Hundred," but only seven were so named. The practice commenced in 1875 and was discontinued three years later because the management decided it was not good sales policy to suggest that different grades of gun were being produced.

15. *Told in* SIDEWINDER.

16. *Told in* HELL IN THE PALO DURO *and* GO BACK TO HELL.

17. *How Annie Singing Bear acquired the distinction of becoming a warrior and won her "man-name" is told in* IS-A-MAN.

18. *Told in* WHITE INDIANS.

19. *Told in Part Two, "The Poison and the Cure,"* WANTED! BELLE STARR.

20. *Told in* WHITE STALLION, RED MARE.

21. *Mark Scrapton, a grandson of the Ysabel Kid, served as a member of Company "Z," Texas Rangers, with Alvin Dustine "Cap" Fog and Ranse Smith—grandsons of Captain Dustine Edward Marsden "Dusty" Fog and Mark Counter, respectively—during the Prohibition era. Information about their specialized duties are given in the* Alvin Dustine "Cap" Fog *series.*